MW01612304

# SAVING STACEY

### Florida Veterans: Book Two

## TIFFANI LYNN

Happy Reading!

For information contact Tiffani Lynn at www.tiffanilynn.com

Cover Design by Dar Albert, Wicked Smart Designs

Background Photograph: Sunsets by Steven J.

Editor: Twin Tweaks Editing

Proofreader: Gray Publishing Services

❀ Created with Vellum

## Acknowledgments

Thank you to my amazing family for your love and support. I couldn't keep doing this if it weren't for your support. I love you all more than you'll ever know.

Special thanks goes to Stacey Clyatt for whom this book and heroine are named after. Her generous donation to the Reading Pals Program in Citrus County Florida is what brought us together and I couldn't be more thankful. She is a beautiful person both inside and out and I'm so happy to now call her friend.

To Casey and Katie at Sodium, Richard and Tiffany at Katch 22, and Rick, Christine and Erin Rice at World Fusion thank you for allowing me to bring local authenticity to my book by mentioning your businesses in my story. They are some of my favorite Citrus County originals.

To my TLC Crew... Watch out for that middle glass and remember not to give two turds. Love you guys!

To my readers, thank you for your time and kindness. Your support means the world to me!

*This book is dedicated to my friends Marine Corporal Joshua Langston White and his beautiful wife Brittni. You've seen the horror and the beauty life has to offer in a way most of us haven't but your smiles continue to light up the lives of those around you. Your friendship means so much to me and my family.*

## 1

## Hudson

How many times am I going to end up in this position? Carmen, my pain-in-the-ass ex-wife, keeps dragging me into the depths of Hell. Instead of kicking and screaming though, I simply follow—figuratively, that is—and work on a way to get her out. She's been hooked on smack since my first deployment to Afghanistan. She's not a woman who makes good choices when she's alone, and if I would've been married to her more than five minutes when I deployed the first time, I would've known this about her.

My dumb ass hooked up with her after a wild night at a bar, and within three months we were married. Carmen was sexy, fun and passionate—everything my 21-year-old self thought I wanted. It was only a couple weeks later that I was sent to Afghanistan. When I returned 8 months later, she was nowhere to be found. Our checking account had been cleaned out, along with our apartment—minus a ton of trash. Fearing something terrible had happened, I went to the police and found out this wasn't uncommon. A lot of young women who marry Marines or soldiers fall into a wild crowd when their husbands are deployed and never come out of it. The police told me that she was likely with a new boyfriend or on the streets, squatting somewhere and high as a kite.

You have no idea what that kind of knowledge does to a man, especially a young man who thinks he's in love. A young man coming home from his first deployment away from his new wife…thinking it's going to be days of sex and sweet kisses from a beautiful woman he can't get enough of, only to find out she's a serious drug addict who bled him dry and took off before he could even get one welcome-home kiss. It was bad enough that my deployment sucked: men in my platoon had died and my mind was a mess from the whole experience. Add Carmen's shit to it and I've never been the same.

The three years we were married were rocky as hell. Bouncing between another long deployment and her in and out of rehab twice more. Those were the worst three years of my life. I've been out of the Navy for two years and life has been better for me, except on the nights I get these calls.

Mike Wade, my partner at Sunset Security, asked me once why I stayed with her after that first deployment. Looking back on things, I'm not 100 percent sure. At the time, I thought staying with her and trying to get her clean was what I was supposed to do. For better or worse and all that, but when I found her trading her body for drugs, I decided that was it. For me—that was too much. Not only was she cheating on me, she was also putting my health at risk. I was done; so I left her and filed for divorce.

Thirty minutes ago I got a call from Carmen saying she was scared and being held against her will in a crack house down on Eighth Avenue. I debated with myself for 10 minutes about whether I should go or give her the tough-love option, but I decided that I wouldn't be able to sleep if I ignored her plea for help. At this point, I hate her for even making me choose.

Crystal River is the cool little town we live in. This place is a combination of small hometown warmth, mixed with kitschy touristy spots. Most of the town is great, with decent neighborhoods, some small farms and older areas with the old Florida cracker-style homes, but it still has one area about a mile from the actual river that's known well by the police because of the heavy drug activity. Eighth Avenue is the main drag in that troubled little neighborhood.

As much as Carmen makes me angry and I want to tell her to go to Hell, I can't; I still feel like she's my responsibility. Every time I ride to her rescue she lives to breathe another day. I knew when I relocated back to this town a couple months ago that Carmen calling was going to be an issue, but I was hoping it wouldn't be this bad.

Tonight, though, I think I should've listened to my gut instinct and stayed down in Tampa. This might be one of the worst places she's been in so far. I'm not sure it's even safe for me to walk inside and breathe the fumes of this place. The address she gave me belongs to a 1970's era, single-wide trailer with a set of broken-down wooden steps leading to the only door in and out of the place. The windows are boarded up and crude graffiti marks the entire outside paneling.

A set of glowing eyes, low to the ground, barely concealed by the trash lying around the edge of the trailer, follow me as I make my way to the door. I'm certain by the size of them it's a cat, but I can't tell how big it is and I'm wishing I would've brought a stick with me in case I have to fight a rabid beast off of me.

I pull my 9mm from the waistband of my pants and grip it tightly in my right hand, ready for anything inside this shithole. When I open the door, one candle burning on a table in the corner gives the place an eerie glow. The walls are lined with faux-wood paneling and a couple of nails mark spots where there used to be pictures, but nothing is displayed there now.

3

One broken curtain rod, sans curtain, hangs slanted precariously above a window, and the missing curtain is nowhere in sight. A grungy, skinny guy—who doesn't even look up at me—is seated on the floor of the kitchen next to the cabinets, melting something in a spoon. Glancing around with ill-disguised disgust, I take in bodies draped all over the place, either completely dazed or passed out. The odor in here is a combo of urine, feces, dirty skin and a sharp medicinal scent. It's disgusting, but not uncommon for the places I'm used to finding Carmen in. *Fuck, I hate this!* I put another tally mark next to the list in my head that denotes instances of wishing I'd never met her.

None of the faces are familiar, so I creep down the hall carefully to avoid the holes under foot that pepper the rotten hallway floorboards. I get the impression everything under me could give way at any moment. There are only three doors in the hallway, so I start with the first one and find it's a bathroom. A dude is lying in the dirty bathtub, fully clothed and sleeping, so I close the door and continue down the hallway. The second door ends up revealing what I'm looking for.

Carmen's emaciated figure is hunched over on the floor in the corner. Her once shiny onyx hair is now dull and ratty, like she doesn't own a brush or even care, but because I've found her like this before, I recognize the oversized, dirty, long-sleeved floral shirt she's wearing. *That damn shirt is so filthy it could probably stand on its own if she took it off.*

Keeping my back to the wall I continue around the room, noting the naked, skin-and-bones man on the bed. One arm and one leg are hanging off the side and his shriveled-up pecker is right out in the open. *If I have to, I can use it for target practice, so he better not move.*

I squat down next to Carmen. "Carm, come on. Wake up! Let's go!" I whisper loudly, hoping to wake her without disturbing the freak on the bed. When she doesn't respond, I shake her a little and she lifts groggy eyes to look at me. "Come on, Carm, let's get out of here."

*Shit, gone is the frantic woman from the phone call, replaced with a woman who has recently shot some kind of life-draining drug into her system. My guess is the asshole on the bed gave her a hit when she freaked out, found a phone, and called me.*

"Can't," she mumbles and lowers her head to her knees again. *This woman is maddening!*

"Why did you call me to come get you if you weren't going to leave when I got here?"

"Didn't know I was gonna be chained. Besides, I'm feeling okay now."

*Spoken like a true junkie.* "Get up, Carm. I'm not fucking around. We're leaving." She lifts her head to look at me again and it lolls back against the wall, exposing the ratty-ass studded dog collar with a chain leading from around her neck all the way back to the bed. The other end is attached to a cuff on the naked dude's wrist. I swear, every time I bail her out of a bad situation the next one is always worse. I'm hoping it can't get worse than this one. I don't know what's worse than this and for her sake I don't want to know.

"Put your head back down and let me unhook the collar."

"No, he'll kill me if he wakes up. I owe him," she slurs.

"How much?" I growl. I hate her and I loathe that I feel obligated to rescue her from these messes she gets into.

Her head lolls forward like she's falling asleep and I shake her. Her eyes blink open as she answers, "A couple of G's."

"Fuck, Carm. Why do you do this to yourself?" I would shake her senseless if I thought it would help, but it won't. It may make me feel better, but nothing is going to help her.

"Screw you, Mr. High and Mighty." The last part is not as insulting as it was meant to be since it's delivered on another slur.

"Yeah, I hear you. I can't leave you here though. Either you lean forward so I can take the damn collar off or I will take the end off the asshole in the bed, which might wake him up. Your choice, but you have about five seconds to make that choice," I hiss at her, wondering why I even bother.

"I never shoulda called you. If he didn't have guys coming over to take a run at me I woulda just stayed here. The last time they gave me some STD and I ended up at the free clinic."

*Gross.* Clenching my teeth hard enough to crack the damn things I pull her forward a little too hard, causing her to cry out. Behind me, the guy on the bed stirs.

"Hey, man! Back off my bitch!" His words are slurred, just like hers, but clear enough to understand.

"Fuck you," I bark back.

Quickly, I work to free her, pull her up to a standing position and shove her behind me. The skinny, naked asshole stands up in all his glory and comes toward me like he can actually do something. This guy must be on some serious shit because he doesn't seem the slightest bit scared. I've got a good hundred pounds of muscle on him and all my brain cells functioning. He doesn't have a shot in hell of getting her from me. I pull the gun out and put it between us so that he can see it, just to make sure he knows I mean business.

"You better back the fuck off! She's walking out of here with me and you're going to forget you know her or I'll make your life a living hell. I won't kill ya; that would be too easy. I'll spread it on the street that you've been narking to the boys on the Sheriff's office. I know enough of them to use names and my story will be accurate enough to believe."

Skinny stops in-place and attempts to look around me to Carmen, but I block his view.

"Eyes to me, asshole. Forget you know her. Chalk this time with her up to a bad mistake. Don't talk to her, don't give her smack, or money, or anything else. She ceases to exist for you."

"You can't tell me what to do." He steps up to me like he's got some balls, which I can see he really *doesn't*.

Quicker than he expects, I grab him by the neck and take him to the mattress. I linger close enough to smell his meth breath. "Last warning, motherfucker. *Back off* and forget you know her." He claws and flails as I cut off his airway. I back off just enough to get an answer and he coughs and wheezes.

"You gonna be done with her?"

"Yeah, man. Fuck you and that dirty bitch."

He obviously didn't think I was serious. I punch him in the face for good measure and blood sprays everywhere.

Rapidly, I back away, grab Carmen and drag her through the bedroom door, down the hallway. Two men of the same variety as the skinny meth head I just walked away from stop us in the living room before we can get to the door and I know this is who he was waiting on.

"Hey, Carmen. Where ya think you're going?" One of them leers at her and I gag a little when I get a look at his almost nonexistent, rotting teeth. *God, she's gone so much farther downhill by even just being in the same house with these people.*

"She's coming with me. Unless you want the same fate as that skinny fucker in the bedroom, you'd better turn and take your ass back where you came from."

"Who da fuck ya think ya are?"

"I'm her husband, jackass."

"Yeah right, dirty Carmen doesn't have a husband. She's the Eighth Avenue whore."

That pretty much snaps my barely holding temper and I charge them both, taking one down and knocking the other to the side hard enough that he slams into the table with the candle. The little light extinguishes and everything goes dark. We wrestle for a few moments until I'm back on my feet. Hastily, I make my way toward the door the best I can in the dark and yell, "Get outside, Carm!" I hear her bare feet scurry toward the door across the squeaky, brittle floor and when the door opens, enough light from the street lamp outside pours in for me to see.

The asshole I knocked into the table has gotten up and is following her. The one I took to the ground isn't moving. I jump up and charge the other guy, diving through the door and on top of him, taking him to his back on the patch of dirt outside the trailer, just past the broken stairs. Several of his fragile bones break under my 230 pounds of weight as we hit the ground. The crunch is almost sickening. I wasn't kidding when I said I have over 100 pounds of muscle on these boys.

Carmen, who was knocked sideways when I hit the guy, screams and scrambles away as I jump to my feet ready to take on anyone else who might be coming at me, but there isn't anyone. Only Carmen and oddly enough, a woman holding a scraggly multicolored cat close to her chest. Cat lady is really out of place. The look of her doesn't match the rest of the low-income ladies around these parts. Her shortage of makeup, absence of fried blond hair and lack of cheap, trashy clothes are the most obvious signs. Her narrowed dark eyes watch me, and she backs away slowly like she's afraid I'm coming after her next. The cat makes a weird noise, much like a scream. Carmen looks between the two of us like she's lost and I finally speak.

"Lady, you don't look like you belong here. Please tell me you aren't looking to score something." I've seen it before. This is how the high class fall low. They come to this part of town looking to score some drugs for a party and the next thing you know they're living on the street and sucking dick to get their next hit. It's a sad and all too common an occurrence.

Her head jerks like I slapped her. "No!" She's both adamant and slightly scared, if the tremble in her lower lip is anything to go by. She holds the cat closer like she's protecting it and herself, which only makes it scream again and I flinch; *That's an awful noise.*

"My cat ran away. I was trying to find it and somehow, it ended up here," she huffs, obviously offended.

"You live near here?"

"That's not your business!"

"Lady, I could give two turds where you live, but this doesn't look like your part of town and the only people coming to this crappy trailer are people looking for drugs or a cheap piece of ass."

"I'm looking for neither." Her lips are pursed and her eyes narrow more as she clings to that noisy cat.

"Well then, get your cat and get the hell out of here."

"That's what I was trying to do," she takes a few steps backwards as she finishes, "before you people started fighting in front of me."

*What kind of idiot hangs out in this neighborhood if she isn't in this life? One that probably really is in the life. Whatever. If she wants to ruin it with drugs or hooking, I certainly won't lose sleep about it.*

I grab Carmen by the arm and pull her toward my truck. "Get in the truck, Carmen."

She stumbles and fights me a little like she's considering it. She knows what's about to happen. I warned her the last time.

"No choice now, Carm. You either go back inside for a gang bang with the meth brothers or you do things my way. I'm done bailing you out."

"I can't."

"Yeah, you can. But not here. You need to go home to Gene and Myrtle in order to do it. I'll take you there, but this is where you decide: live or die."

The waterworks start and tears begin pouring from her eyes like they have a hose attached to them. I've seen and heard it all from her, so I know this is part fear and part manipulation. *I have to stick to my guns. No matter how much it bothers me to see a woman cry.* "Get in the truck. I've got a job in the morning and need to get you settled before that. If I'm driving to the Alabama line tonight, I need to go now."

She rests her forehead on the door of my truck and I wait for 30 seconds before I prompt her again. "Come on, Carm. Don't break your mama's heart again. Do it for her. She already lost Leslie."

It's not a minute later when I'm driving out of there with Carmen curled up in the passenger seat balling her eyes out. I dial Gene's number and his voice rings out through my truck since I have the Bluetooth on.

"Everything okay, Hudson?"

"Bringing your daughter home. She's in a bad way. See if you can get her into a rehab tonight or in the morning or she'll be gone again. I'll meet you in Defuniak Springs in four and a half hours at that Walmart parking lot, right off of I-10."

"Thanks, Hudson." Her father's voice is tired and he's not even bothering to ask questions. He came looking for her once, a few months ago, and asked for my help. Once we found her she wouldn't leave with him—and she was only half this bad—so he has an idea of what he's going to get. I hate it for him. Gene's a good man, a hard-working, God-fearing man who loves his family beyond measure. When his youngest daughter died in a car accident a year out of high school, their family fell apart. When I married Carmen a year later, Gene hoped I would be the answer to his prayers for Carm, but instead it only got worse.

"Anything, Gene. You know it."

Not wanting to drag this out any further, I hang up and head north up Highway 19. Instead of thinking about Carmen and the mess she got herself into this time, I think about the too-good-for-Eighth ̄Avenue cat lady. *Why in the hell would a woman who looks like her be living in that part of town and running around at night? It had to be obvious to her that the neighborhood is one you don't wander in during the day and especially not after dark. Makes no sense.*

## 2

## Stacey

This damn cat is going to be the death of me. I survived Lawson's beatings only to stumble into an equally crappy situation chasing after her. As much as I'd like to say screw the cat, I can't. I named her Screamer and naming her makes a difference. Everyone knows you should never name an animal unless you plan to keep it, so I'm keeping her. She got the name because she screams when she's irritated. This crazy, loud-mouthed cat has been my only friend since I arrived three weeks ago and can be my only friend as long as I'm on the run. I need to keep a low profile until the police find Lawson, because if he finds me first...he's going to kill me this time.

The big guy wasn't wrong. I'm in a horrible part of town, but picking the worst part of this little town to rent a place was done on purpose. Number one, because the rent is cheap, and number two, because Lawson would never think to look for me here, even if he tracked me to this town—which I don't think he can do. When I ran, I didn't take any credit or debit cards. I have a new burner cell phone and a used, but new-to-me, car that I bought with cash, which leaves no way to trace me. I'd spent a lot of time planning for this and I wasn't going to make a silly mistake and be easily found. I've managed to be gone for six months without being discovered, so I've done something right.

I love it here; well, maybe not this particular neighborhood, but this town…I love. Even the name, Crystal River, is nice. Other than these couple of streets, it's a pretty place with friendly people, and best of all they have manatees. I've been in love with the gentle giants since I was a kid. My grandpa brought me here on vacation when I was seven, while my mother was sick, after my dad left us, and it's been my happy place ever since. For once, I'm glad that Lawson was too self-centered to learn enough about my life to know it even exists in the confines of my memory. If I can find a way to stay here forever, I will.

Today, my goal is to find a job. I'm hoping if I explain my situation to someone, they'll let me work off the books until I can get this all resolved. The Lobster Lounge is my first stop. It's a new little restaurant located along Kings Bay and it's hopping every day. I have just enough money to make it for two more months the way I'm going without working. I've been very careful with my money, but I don't want it to run out so that I end up living on the streets. Florida is a warm place most of the year, but the afternoon storms freak me out and I can't imagine trying to keep all my stuff dry while living outside. I hear there are homeless communities in the woods near the river, but I've also heard they aren't safe for single women, so that will be a last resort.

It's interesting how that guy last night who came tumbling out of the crack house where I found Screamer was built similarly to Lawson—muscular and thick, like an NFL linebacker —and when I first saw him a sliver of fear zipped up my spine. My first instinct was to run as hard and as fast as I could, but he turned toward me and spoke before I could physically react, letting me know that it wasn't Lawson. This man was more handsome, in a rugged kind of way, whereas Lawson was bulky but preppy with soft hands. There is no way that man from last night has soft hands. He's rough in all the best ways a man can be, but he's also someone who takes care of himself. Guys like him don't usually come out of places like the crack trailer, so I'm guessing he was retrieving the woman who came out of the trailer before him. *I wonder if she's his girlfriend or sister or what.* She was obviously eaten up with drugs. She had the typical look of a woman on crack or meth—filthy skin and clothes, missing teeth, and hair that hasn't seen a brush in a very long time.

Judging by the scrawny, limp guy on the ground that the big guy crushed coming out the door when they left, the big guy wasn't too happy to be there. I wanted to laugh and at the same time yell at the big guy when he was questioning me. I'm obviously no crackhead and probably fit in around these streets about as well as Hillary Clinton in one of her pantsuits would. I find my reaction to him puzzling though. After what I went through with Lawson, I should be terrified of someone the big guy's size with a pissy attitude, but something about him left me feeling like he wouldn't hurt me. It could be naiveté, or it could be intuition. Luckily, he didn't stick around for me to find out.

THE NEXT MORNING, I brush my hair and tug it back into a sleek ponytail, pull on a collared golf shirt and a decent pair of jeans and set off to find a job. I left all of my fancy clothes behind when I ran, and although those were part of who I was for a long time, it feels better to be the original me in comfortable clothes for a change.

ALTHOUGH I PUT in my application at a few places within a couple of hours, only the Lobster Lounge would consider hiring me without documentation for a few months. It's my first choice, so that's good. If I want to stay on longer than that, I need to get on the books, but the owner was awesome and when I explained my story to him, without using names or where I came from, he agreed to give me a few months of work. I almost cried I was so happy. He tossed me a black server apron with a cartoonish red lobster on the front and within minutes I became the newest waitress at the Lobster Lounge.

My first shift will be tonight, training with a woman named Lola, who the owner warned me wasn't the most patient person, but definitely the most skilled at her job. He told me to have a thick skin and pay attention. Mr. Clark has no idea what it is to have a thick skin like I do. Nothing will ever be as bad as what I endured with Lawson's physical and verbal abuse. I think I can face almost anything after three years of that.

On my way home I swing by the grocery store and pick up more food for Screamer and a box of chocolate Hostess snack cakes to celebrate my good news. *Happy* doesn't even begin to describe me, but for the first time in weeks I'm a little lonely, realizing that I have no one other than a feral cat to share my smile with. Not that I had anyone left up home.

When I married Lawson, the only family I had was dead and he made sure any friends close to me backed off. After a while my girlfriends stopped calling, even when he wasn't around. None of them could understand why I stayed. It's not that I wanted to, hell, he was a scary son of a bitch, but I had nowhere to go that wouldn't put someone I cared about in danger. When I say he's crazy, I don't mean a little bit. The threats he made to me were scarier than some of the scariest movies I've ever seen. I figured if a man could think up the things he threatened to do to my friends and their husbands, then he was probably likely to do them too.

———

TWO WEEKS into my new job, I'm on the second half of a double shift when the big guy from the crack trailer enters. It's the set of his jaw and his stance in the doorway that give him away. Even if I didn't hear the timbre of his voice, I'd know it's the same guy. The term good-looking doesn't do him justice when the lights are on though. The man is huge. Broad shoulders, a small but broad nose, a scar that runs up from his right eyebrow and disappears under his baseball cap, thick muscles from head to toe and a demeanor that says don't fuck with me. The man he's with is taller than him, with leaner muscles and a more relaxed way about him.

The taller guy flashes an easy smile at the hostess, who blushes under his attention and leads them to a table in my section. *Great.* My only saving grace is that it was dark the night I found Screamer outside the trailer where I met him, so he shouldn't even recognize me. I take a swallow of my water that's hidden behind the drink station, pull my pen from where I shoved it above my ear and waltz over, hoping to appear laid-back.

"Evenin', guys, I'm Stacey; I'll be your server tonight." I greet them without eye contact, pretending to be jotting something down on my order pad, but really I'm avoiding Mr. Muscles' eyes. "What can I get y'all to drink?"

"Coors draft," they both answer in unison.

"Okay, I'll be right back with those. Fried catfish fillets are the special tonight."

As I'm walking away, I hear Mr. Muscles ask, "When is Summer coming home? It's been too long since I've seen her."

"Probably a week."

The rest of their conversation fades away as I approach the bar and place their order. The bartender, Nick, is about 10 years older than I am and married, but it hasn't stopped him from flirting with me constantly. I was ready to tell him to back off when his wife showed up and slid up on a barstool for a beer one night. While he continued to flirt with me and the other waitresses, my concern must have been obvious because she told me not to worry about it. "He's harmless and has been doing it for years," was her exact quote. So far, she's been right; he's harmless.

When I grab both beers and turn toward their table, I notice Mr. Muscles is staring at me like he's trying to figure something out. There's no way he would know who I am so I ignore the shiver of fear it gives me.

I place the beers in front of them and pull my pad back out of my apron. "What can I get you guys to eat?"

The tall one answers first, "The catfish sounds good." I study him and realize he's at least 10 years older than Mr. Muscles, but he's aging in that way men do where they only become more handsome. Once I realize that I'm staring awkwardly, I turn my attention to Mr. Muscles and he answers, "All-you-can-eat shrimp. By the way, how's your noisy-ass cat?"

My eyes jump from my pad to his face. "What do you mean?"

The tall one smacks him in the chest. "Hudson, don't be a dick."

Mr. Muscles, who is apparently named Hudson, turns to glare at his friend. "What the hell do you think I'm asking her? I saw her the other night when I pulled Carmen out of another shithole and she was retrieving her cat that ran away."

I release an annoyed sigh. "She's fine. I just keep her away from the door now so she can't run out."

"Probably a good idea in that neighborhood, but if she

does get out again, let her go. All kinds of bad shit goes down over there. Would hate for you to get caught in the crossfire."

"Um...thanks. I'll keep that in mind." Not knowing what else to say I turn and move to the kitchen to put their orders in. As I'm walking away, I hear the tall one ask Hudson, "I thought you cut Carmen loose a while ago?"

"I did, but she keeps calling and I can't leave her in those situations. She's in bad shape. This time I took her to her dad in Alabama and told her not to come back. Let's hope she listens."

I'm glad he's not her pimp. In that neighborhood, looking like she did, it wouldn't have surprised me. Not that I should care. In fact, I shouldn't be paying attention at all. The lower the profile I keep, the better for me. Getting involved with anyone, even on a friendly level, puts me at risk, and Hudson has no hope of being low profile. When he walks into a room, everyone notices. He's just that kind of guy.

I see to my other tables, get the guys new beers as they finish the last ones and bring their food out once it's ready. I don't linger and I certainly don't flirt, even though the thought of it crosses my mind for the first time in a long time. If there was ever a guy made to my exact specifications, it's him. At least on the outside. I have no idea what he's like on the inside. He could be a complete prick like Lawson turned out to be and I would be none the wiser at this point. But I've always had a thing for big guys. Maybe it's the way they make me feel tiny and feminine when they're next to me, or the fact that no one usually messes with them because of the way they look on the outside.

———

LATER THAT NIGHT, when the restaurant is mostly empty and my side work is done, I cash out and say goodbye to the remaining barflies who are perched on their stools at the bar. I normally don't stop on the way home, but this time I feel like a treat so I stop at Walgreens to grab a pint of ice cream. It's the only store open at this hour, other than a few sketchy gas stations, and my sweet tooth is working overtime.

I hustle into the store, grab and pay for my treat and return to my car. I pull my seat belt across my lap, locking it into place, and turn the key in the ignition. Click, click, click is the only sound the car makes. I try again. Same result. Frustration crawls under the surface of my skin and digs at my nerves. Twisting the key one more time while begging, out loud, for it to start up, I get the same result.

*Son of a bitch! I just drove it over here with no issue. Why in the hell would it die now?* I try it again, pumping the gas this time, hoping that will do the trick. It doesn't. *Shit. I don't want to call a tow truck and have to sit here and wait in this parking lot for at least an hour. Sure, it's a small town, and it may not take that long, but this is also my life, which means luck won't be in my favor.*

I pull out my cell phone to call for a cab. My rental isn't far from here but walking through that neighborhood at this time of night is asking to be mixed up in a drive-by shooting or harassed by a gang of troublemaking teenagers. Neither of which sounds appealing.

Grabbing my phone, I climb out of the car with my purse and see if I can get the address on the building. I type 411 into my phone to get the number for a taxi and before I hit send the headlights of a truck come across the parking lot and practically blind me as they pull in. The vehicle slides in next to mine and I take a step back. *This whole lot is empty, why would that person pull in next to me?* Fear winds its way through my muscles and into my gut. Such a familiar and unwelcome feeling. I take a few more steps back, preparing myself to run if I need to. About that time the passenger-side window rolls down and the somewhat-familiar deep voice of Hudson calls out. "Hey,

Stacey. You okay? You shouldn't be standing out here alone at this hour. This is a nice town but after a certain time, no place is safe."

I can't help the sigh of relief that comes from my lungs or the slight irritation that bubbles up along with it. *Does he think I'm an idiot? That I enjoy putting myself in dangerous situations just because?*

Without thinking, I snap at him. "It's not like I hang out in the Walgreens parking lot for the hell of it. My car won't start."

The window rolls up and the door opens. I hear his boots hit the ground and watch as he leans over the bed of his truck, digging into the silver metal tool box that stretches across a section of the back. A few seconds later he closes the box and saunters around the front of the vehicles.

"Pop your hood and I'll jump you."

I don't know why, especially since he pissed me off less than a minute ago, but his comment strikes me as funny so I giggle a little. I've always had a seventh-grade-boy's sense of humor. Only when I married Lawson did that get hushed and stifled.

Hudson's head pops up and his eyes narrow on me. Normally, even the slight irritation of a man would have me cowering because of Lawson's temper, but with him—and don't ask me why, because I have no idea— with Hudson, I feel more defiant.

"Could you pop the hood so we can get this over with?" he growls, not finding anything funny.

"I didn't tell you that you had to help me. I'll be just fine if you want to climb back in that truck and go back to whatever it was you were doing."

"Lady, I'm not trying to be a dick, but standing in the parking lot for an excessive amount of time when I could easily already have your car jumped and you out of here is a huge waste of time. You might have plenty of it, but I don't."

*This guy has a serious attitude problem. Why would he stop to help me if he doesn't have time to do it?* I prop my hands on my hips and roll my eyes. *Whatever.* "Look, if you have better things to do, just go. I can take care of myself."

"No one in this town knows you. Who you gonna call for help?"

"How would you know that—and why does it matter? If you have somewhere to be, go. I'm a big girl and have been solving my own problems for years without you."

His eyes narrow, his face turns red and I continue to watch as his head practically explodes. Oddly enough, again, I don't cower and apologize like I would have with Lawson. I stand there with my chin raised defiantly and my back straight. I've proven that I can take care of myself and will always find a way to do so.

He drops his head and all I can see is the top of his baseball cap. His shoulders rise and fall like he's taking a few calming breaths and without another word he turns and walks around me to my car door, opens it, and pops the hood. Within a few seconds he has the wires connected, and I still haven't moved. I'm not sure what to do. I want to smack him for being rude to me for no reason, but at the same time I want to hug him for helping me.

Just when I'm ready to say thank you he jogs around the truck, turns the ignition and it powers up. He sits inside for a minute or two before getting out and jogging back around. The look he gives me before he slides behind the wheel of my car is as irritated as they come. My mood grows more sour when he uses every ounce of sarcasm he can muster to ask, "Can I get the keys?"

"Oh, shit," I mumble. I forgot I had them in my hand.

Finally, my feet move from the spot they've been planted and I carry the keys to him. He takes them without a word and within a few seconds my car starts. Relief washes over me and I exhale loudly. I don't want to blow my money on fixing major car problems. Tomorrow I'll buy a new battery, which doesn't cost too much, and go about my business.

Hudson gets out of the car and unhooks the cables before throwing them back in his tool box. Then, without another word, he closes my hood and his, climbs in his truck and pulls away. He didn't even give me a chance to say anything, not even a thank you. What kind of asshole does that? I mean, on one hand, he did stop to help me, but on the other, it was like he really didn't want to do it. It was also like talking to me was painfully irritating and he couldn't be bothered. *Thank goodness I won't have to see him again anytime soon or maybe even at all. He's kind of a jerk.*

THE NEXT MORNING, after a fitful night of sleep, a thumping on my front door wakes me. *Who the hell is at my door? I don't know anyone and no one knows where I live.* Just in case, I grab a knife from my kitchen and grip it tightly in my hand as I check the peephole, only to find a familiar ball cap clearly visible. *Hudson. What is he doing here and how did he find me?*

When I open the door, he doesn't waste time on pleasantries. After his exit yesterday, I wouldn't expect anything else, to be honest. Without any kind of greeting, he blurts, "I need your keys to install the battery."

Still holding tight to the knife with my right hand, I rub my eyes with my left palm, trying to wake up a little in an effort to understand what he's doing here. It's early and I'm not a morning person. "What are you doing here?"

His eyes dart to the knife in my hand before he answers. "Installing your new battery."

"What new battery? I haven't gotten one yet."

It's obvious I'm not comprehending any of this fast enough, if I'm judging by his tightly pursed lips before he responds. "I picked one up. My buddy owns an auto shop and had one on hand. Keys." He wiggles his fingers at me. I stare at his fingers, trying to process all of this. *This scenario is seriously bizarre.*

He didn't say goodbye or anything last night, much less tell me this was his plan, and now he's standing on my porch wanting the keys to my car. I haven't even brushed my teeth or hair yet. I'm certain Medusa has nothing on me.

"You didn't need to do that. How much was the battery?"

"Not much. Can you get me the keys? I've got shit to do and don't have time to go round and round again."

*This guy is infuriating.* "Then why bother?"

"Because I know you'll walk back through this neighborhood to get to work today and that's not cool. Now for the last time, can you get me your keys?"

*How dumb does he think I am? I can handle myself. It would have taken a little bit of work, but I would've figure this out on my own. I don't need him riding—unhappily I might add—to my rescue.*

"Babe," he growls impatiently.

"Fine!" I stomp off to the kitchen to retrieve the keys from the counter. *If letting him handle this will make him go away, then he can have my keys.* I bring them back and drop them in his hand. He turns without another word and marches to my car, cursing the whole way. I go to my room, change my clothes, pull my hair back in a ponytail and slip on some flip-flops, intent on helping him. Pulling money out of my secret hiding place, I shove it in my pocket and head back out.

When I get outside, he almost has it done. If I can't say anything else nice about him, at least I can say he works fast. I grab 100 dollars and pass it to him as he finishes. Hudson stares at my hand like it's a snake ready to bite. I shake it at him a little. "Here, you didn't tell me how much it was so I just guessed. I can grab more if it's more than this." He looks around me at the front of my house and then back at my hand.

With a shake of his head he turns and saunters back to his truck, never saying a word.

"Hudson. You need to take this!" I shout at his retreating back.

"I don't *need* to do nothin'. By the looks of things, you need it more than I do."

Why is this guy such an asshole? Visions of me kicking him between the legs fly through my head. *How can someone be so thoughtful and such a jerk at the same time?*

"You just bought me a battery and installed it for nothing. I can't accept that. Take the damn money. I don't want your charity!"

Ignoring me, he climbs into the truck and something inside me snaps. I storm up to the truck and bang on the window with my fist. His eyes widen a little before he lowers the window. "I'd appreciate it if you didn't break my window."

"Well, then take the money. I'm not a charity case. I don't even know you, and we obviously don't like each other, so it's not like a favor for a friend. Take the damn money!"

He starts to laugh at me, further infuriating me, so I toss the money into the truck and stomp back toward the house. On my way inside I can hear him yell, "Ungrateful woman. Don't even know why I bothered."

My blood boils in my veins and I turn back toward him as I stand on my front porch. "Screw you! I tried to be grateful! I tried to thank you and pay you, but you were too busy being a dick to notice. Why bother doing something nice if you're going to ruin it with a shitty attitude?" I scream. I don't wait to hear his response. I enter my house, slamming the door behind me. *Asshole! I don't even know this guy and he's insulted me several times and been an absolute jerk. I'll be happy if I never have to see him again.*

---

3

## Hudson

---

Stacey is insanely annoying and surprisingly beautiful first thing in the morning. Even with her hair a ratted mess and her eyes sleepy, there's a certain sweet sexuality about her that shines through. Not many women have that, but I do see why she's not married or living with someone. She's got an attitude. Everything I've said or done has lit a fire in her eyes that I'm not used to seeing. Most of the women I'm around are flirty and charming, trying to get, or keep, my attention. The other ones are women I've known for years and have easy friendships with...no drama. I've met Stacey a handful of times and each time she's managed to get under my skin and irritate me.

I should've told her I was bringing her a battery today, but I honestly didn't know it myself. I lie awake last night, worried that she'd walk through that neighborhood to get to the auto parts store to buy it, so I called Howie and picked one up from him. Then when I showed up with it, I thought she'd be grateful, but instead she was pissed. Maybe I was a little bit grumpy —hell, I didn't want to care about her safety when she had to venture out to get a new battery this morning—but I wasn't that heartless either. Stacey was giving me dirty looks as soon as she opened the door. I don't understand women at all. I guess that's how I ended up married to a sneaky, lying, drug-addicted mess.

I pull up Mike's number and hit send. His voice comes through the speakers of my truck.

"What's up, Hudson?"

"We still meeting that client today at 11?" I ask.

"Yeah, then I have to make a run to Tampa and bring up the last load of Summer's stuff. I want it all here when she gets back. Last time, she complained that half her stuff was still down there."

"Okay. I've got surveillance on the Ruffman kid today. So stupid. I could tell the first time I saw him he was up to no good, but if they want to pay us to get them proof, so be it."

"Yeah, that kid's a punk for sure. At least his mom and stepdad are cluing in, rather than pretending he's a good kid."

"Yeah, but let's see if they do anything about it before he knocks up his girlfriend or gets caught in a local drug bust. Knowing these people, they'll hold on to the information we give them and do nothing about it."

"If Don Ruffman wants to run for mayor, then he will. Small towns don't do well with scandal."

"True. I'm going to hit the gym this morning and then I'll see you there at 11. Can we meet somewhere other than the Lobster Lounge?"

"No, this is the client's choice and he was adamant. He's not in town often, but he knows the owner and wants to try it out, so suck it up, buttercup."

I groan and say a silent prayer that Ms. Mouthy is off today. I'm not prepared to deal with more of her attitude. She's already ruined my morning so far.

AT 11 O'CLOCK, I'm walking through the doors of the Lobster Lounge. I worked out, expelling my irritation and pent-up frustration. Now I'm refreshed and ready to eat. We're meeting a client I'm not familiar with, but looking him up online provided a ton of information.

Josiah Brown's a self-made multi-millionaire. His business has something to do with turbines and he's in his mid-40's. He was born in Southern Florida and has homes in New York and Miami but likes to spend a couple of weeks a year here in Crystal River. That's how he found us.

When I approach Mike he's seated at a high-top round table in the bar area; the guy is perpetually early to everything. Me, I'm never late, but I'm rarely early.

I take off my baseball cap and set it in my lap. Mike's in a button-down shirt and jeans, looking a little more professional than my polo, jeans, work boots and baseball cap.

Mike looks over my head. "Hello, Mr. Brown."

I turn to stand and he stops me. "No need to get up. I'm Josiah Brown. Nice to meet you, gentlemen."

We both shake hands and Josiah sits in a chair between us. He waves a waitress over and she says, "I can take your drink order, but Stacey is your server. She'll be over in a moment. What'll you have?"

I audibly groan and Mike's attention jerks my way, his brows pulled tight, obviously confused by my reaction. "Coke," I mumble.

*Why is Stacey working today and why does she have our table? I can't seem to escape her since our paths crossed initially. Up until a couple of weeks ago I'd never seen her before and now she's everywhere I go. If I get attitude from her in front of Mike and the client, I'm not going to be happy.*

"You okay?" Mike asks as the server bounces away.

"Yeah, I'm good." I give him a look indicating that I'll explain later.

"So what can we help you with, Josiah?" Mike asks after taking my hint to change the subject. He does most of the talking at client meetings, and I tend to be the silent show of force. I've never been much of a talker and am more comfortable with him taking the lead with these things.

"I've looked into you guys and I know you recently broke off from Security Six, who come highly recommended."

"Yeah," Mike says cautiously.

"Surprising to me, I gave them a call and they also recommended you. They said they hated to see you go, but understood why you wanted to be based out of Crystal River and will probably be working with you in the future on some things. I follow celebrity news and know that you had a hand in saving Summer Arden."

Mike cuts the guy off, "Wade."

Josiah pauses, startled by Mike's interruption. "Excuse me?"

"Summer Arden Wade. She's my wife now."

Josiah chuckles. "Oh, yeah. Sorry, I didn't realize she took on your name."

"Yeah."

I laugh a little too because when it comes to Summer, Mike is possessive. I guess if it took the woman I loved 35 years to love me back, then I'd probably feel the same. But it's kind of out of character for him to be so abrupt with a client.

Josiah seems to understand and continues. "In case you haven't checked into me yet, I'll tell you that my wife is a supermodel. I met her at a coffee shop in Miami a few years ago and finally convinced her to marry me. The problem now is that her career has taken off and she's traveling more. Most of the time I can go with her and make sure that proper security measures are taken, but I have a few conflicting dates and need someone I can trust to stay with her to make sure she's safe.

She's had a few kidnapping threats and I won't trust just anyone."

"Hudson and Thomas, who is my brother and an employee, can travel with her. My wife is pregnant so I won't be traveling much for the next six to nine months. If it's after that timeframe, then I can do it. We will need to talk specifics if you agree to our standard contract, but it's definitely something we can do. I have to ask though—why did you choose us? You're from Miami and I know of a couple groups down there that do the same thing."

"I wanted a small company, one that I was certain would focus on her safety. With some of the others she won't be their biggest client and that could mean sloppy work. She's the light of my life and I won't trust just anyone. I also want hands-on service without it being...how do I say this delicately?" His right eyebrow raises before he finishes. "Too hands-on. The biggest company in Miami has a history of hooking up with their clients. I don't want to worry in more ways than one. I checked into you both and your integrity is known far and wide. Bottom line...I trust you."

Hooking up with the clientele? Yes, I have heard that's a problem for some. I never cross work with pleasure, won't even allow myself to consider it, and Mike is so eaten up with Summer he hasn't noticed a single pretty face in his vicinity for a while now. Thomas isn't interested in settling down at all and never mixes work and pleasure. Sunset Security is a right fit for this job if those are concerns.

"Sorry, guys, I'm running a little slow today," a familiar voice says like she's out of breath. *Damn.* I don't even look up from my menu because I know I'll find Stacey standing there.

"I'll have the special," Josiah says.

"Make that two," Mike says.

"I'll have the shrimp platter," I answer as I pass her the menu and find her scowling at me.

It almost makes me laugh how irritated she seems to be. Mike glances between us as we stare each other down. The smattering of cute little freckles on her nose is more prominent today, like it was when I woke her up this morning, and as I search her face I realize she hasn't put on any makeup. *She's apparently one of those rare women who looks just as beautiful without makeup as she does with it. Damn it! I don't even need to be thinking about what she looks like.* I turn my face away and attempt to focus on anything but her.

"It shouldn't take long, guys. The kitchen is moving steady today. I'll check on you in a few minutes," she says before she turns on her heel and walks away.

We make it through our meeting and the rest of lunch with me doing a good impression of a man not paying any attention to Stacey. It works for the most part and when it's time to leave I drop an extra 20 bucks on the table because it's obvious by where she lives that she needs it, and let's face it, she's a good server. Or at least that's what I tell myself.

I know deep down that I have a problem. I have a pathological desire to care for people in need, women especially, and she seems like a woman who requires some looking after. Her attitude with me screams, 'I can take care of myself,' but there is a vulnerability I've seen pass through her eyes a few times that just calls to a man like me. *I need to stay out of this restaurant and keep my distance from her. The last woman I was involved with for more than one night had to be pulled out of a crack trailer and delivered to another state, so I'm not in the mood to deal with any more drama. I need to be focused on work and building our business, not on needy women.*

When we're back at our office on Citrus Avenue, Mike sits in one of the chairs across from me and props his feet up on my desk. I hate it when he does that, but he's doing it just to piss me off and I refuse to take the bait.

"So—" he drags it out and I continue typing, filling in the

blanks on the contract for Josiah. "You going to tell me about the Lobster Lounge lady?"

"Nothing to tell."

"If I believed that, I wouldn't be in your office looking for answers like a high school BFF the day after prom," Mike comments with a wide smile.

I open my mouth to respond, but don't look up from what I'm doing, and Mike stops me before any words can come out.

"Don't even try to feed me a line of bullshit. What's the deal? I wouldn't be surprised if she spit in your food before she brought it out to you, and don't think I didn't notice the extra 20 dollars you left for her."

"Do you miss anything?" I ask, annoyed with how much he picked up on.

He gestures for me to move along with my explanation and I sigh.

"Look, I met her when I grabbed Carmen out of the last crack house."

"Yeah, you told me that." His smile never fades. He's getting way too much enjoyment out of this.

"Then I saw her at Walgreens last night at one in the morning and her car wouldn't start and then I gave her a jump to get her home. This morning I took her a new battery and installed it so she wouldn't have to walk to work through that shitty neighborhood because I knew her car wouldn't start without help. She needed a new one. I also didn't know if she had the money to get it."

Mike's eyebrow quirks up, his unspoken question lingering between us. *How is that your problem?*

"Don't look at me like that. Eighth Avenue is a scary little area. She doesn't belong over there and I couldn't sleep thinking about her walking those streets to get where she needed to go."

His hands go up. "Hey, man, I didn't say anything about it;

I'm all for helping out someone in need, especially a woman. I am wondering though—why, if you did such a nice thing for her, did she look like she wanted to punch you in the nuts?"

"I may have showed up at her place early and not been very friendly about it."

"Why go to all that trouble to impress her and then act like a dick?"

"I wasn't trying to impress her." I scowl at him. "I was trying to help someone in need."

"Who happens to look like a mixture of Mila Kunis and Minka Kelly. Sure. Feed me another line."

"Don't be an ass. You know about Carmen. You know I've got no room for a crazy, broke woman who is constantly in need of something. And Stacey screams that loud and clear."

"Something doesn't match up. I'm not so sure she's who you think she is. Don't ask me why I feel that way, but my gut tells me that things aren't exactly how they appear. Maybe you should give it a shot. Try being nice to her for once and that may help."

He has no idea how dangerous that is for me. If I let someone like her into my life, I'll end up like I was after that first deployment—penniless and heartbroken. Not going to happen. I don't care what her story is. I don't care why a beautiful, obviously out-of-place woman is living in the ghetto of this town. The only thing I care about is staying away from a troubled situation. I did my good deed and can now sleep at night.

# 4

## Stacey

Muscles, thick thighs, beefy arms and wide shoulders. Can't forget the beat-up gray and light blue SFG baseball cap he always wears either. I don't even know what SFG is, but the fact that he's always wearing it makes me want to know what that is. Of the list of things that come to mind about him, the hat was not a prominent feature, nor the last thing I saw before my eyes flew open at five-thirty this morning. I dreamt of him all night long.

Damn that man! I can't figure him out. He has the thoughtfulness of a Sunday school teacher and the personality of a rattlesnake. He left me 20 bucks, plus a regular tip, which is really sweet. I know it was him because I saw him return to the table when the other two guys were walking out ahead of him. He thinks because I live in this shithole, I need the money. I want to be pissed at the guy for treating me like a charity case, because I'm not, but I can't ignore the warmth that sat in my belly when I thought about the nice things he's done since I first saw him.

Determined to push him out of my mind, I slip on my workout wear gear and snag my keys and earbuds from the counter. I drive my car down to Citrus Avenue and park in front of the Irish pub. *No one will be there this early or care that I'm parked here.* After a brief stretch, I place my headphones in my ears and put on my running playlist. Then I jog down to the trail and commence wearing myself out. After only a couple of miles, I'm gassed. The humidity and heat around here are stifling this time of year. I don't know what I was thinking. In South Carolina, I ran almost 10 miles a day. Of course, I was literally preparing to run from my husband if necessary, but I haven't been exercising since I left.

With my hands on my hips I walk as fast as my tired legs will carry me the couple of blocks back to my car. I pop the trunk and wipe my face with the towel that I leave in there for emergencies and make a mental note to replace the towel with a clean one after I go to the Laundromat. I pull a half-empty water bottle from the floorboard of my passenger side and finish it off, cursing myself for not bringing more.

When I close my trunk a weird tingly feeling slides down my neck, like when someone is watching me. I turn in every direction, looking to see who it could be. The town is still quiet at this hour and I don't see anyone around. There are cars driving down Highway 19, which is a block away but not much else is going on. I can't see anyone and my unease grows, so I get inside my car and drive back home, making sure to take the long way there and watch my rearview for anyone who might be following me.

The rest of the day isn't much better. The feeling that someone is watching me never quite goes away and I end up eating the last can of baked beans and the heel of the bread for a late lunch. I was supposed to go to the grocery store, but I was too afraid to leave for fear Lawson had found me. Tomorrow is going to prove tricky when I'm supposed to go to work, because I'm too afraid to leave the house.

AFTER ANOTHER FITFUL night of sleep, this one different than the night before, I finally pull myself together to go to work. While brushing my teeth I stare into the mirror and remind myself why I ran, why I'm worth saving, and how I can't stay cooped up in the house worried that he's finally found me. He took my life from me once and I won't let it happen again. I just wish the police would find him so I could stop freaking myself out.

THANK goodness work is busy tonight because it makes the time go by quickly. Only Nick seems to notice my nervousness, but he doesn't say anything until I jump three feet into the air when he comes up behind me in the hallway leading to the cooler.

He places both hands on my shoulders to steady me. "Hey, Stacey. Calm down. I'm not going to hurt you. I'm trying to get the Bud Light from the walk-in cooler. For some reason these contractors love that shit."

I allow my heart rate to settle before I lift my head and meet his eyes. "Sorry, I've been a little jumpy. I just got a weird feeling yesterday after my run, like someone was watching me, and I haven't felt right since. I need to get over it."

"The only person watching you all night has been me. Now, the place is still hoppin' so get your ass back on the floor." He pats my shoulder and winks to let me know he's being silly.

"You're right. I know I'm paranoid. See you out there." I turn and head back to see how my tables are doing.

Despite my claim to Nick that I'm being paranoid, I don't think I am. The later my shift goes, the worse it gets. Almost to the point that I'm ready to drop the tray from my hand and run again. I can't stand this sitting-duck feeling I have. If Lawson gets his hands on me this time, the gravedigger can go ahead and get his backhoe ready because Lawson won't let me live to see another day. He threatened murder every time he took his fists to me. He told me that if I shared what was going on with anyone that it would be the last thing I ever did. The last beating was bad enough that I figured if he did kill me, it would be worth it not to ever live in that kind of pain and fear again.

As I clear one of my last tables for the night, I'm second-guessing my need to get a job. Wondering why I couldn't try to live on my cash a little bit longer. This job made my face familiar in this area and if he does come in here for some reason and shows my picture around, someone will recognize me and point him in my direction. In fact, maybe that's already happened.

I set the dirty dishes near the dishwasher area and rested my hip against the counter as I contemplated what I should do. I don't want to run again. I'll have to start over and burn even more money moving into a new place. I enjoy coming to work every day and not looking at my walls with nothing to do. I need to figure out if I'm really being watched or not. After that I can figure out my next move. I'm just not sure how to do that, other than growing eyes in the back of my head, which is obviously not feasible.

As I'm chewing my nail and considering my options, Nick leans in the doorway. "Hey, there's someone out here asking for you."

My heart rate kicks up. "I don't know anyone here."

"Well, he knows you."

"Did you get a name? What does he look like?" My palms begin itching as sweat gathers on my brow and fear settles in my gut like a heavy stone.

"Kinda tall, a little on the rough side. Weird hazel eyes.

Leathery skin. A shaggy brown mullet. Never seen him in here before." He shrugs and studies me.

That's not Lawson. No, Lawson is a big guy and muscular, but very clean-cut. He's always wearing a collared shirt and expensive shorts and boat shoes if he's not working out. He also has perfectly coiffed short hair and he moisturizes too much to have leathery skin. But my guess is it's someone Lawson sent looking for me; he would hire someone who looked like that to come sniff me out.

"Nick, wait here for a minute or two and then go back and tell him I must be in the bathroom. That should give me enough time to get out the back." I strip off my apron and pass it to him.

"What's going on, Stacey?"

"Nothing I can talk about now. I'll explain later, but please just do this for me. I'll be in touch. I can't finish my shift. Call Mr. Clark and tell him what just happened. He will understand why I'm leaving now."

He shakes his head, his eyes weary as they study me for a second too long. "What's going on, Stacey? If you're in trouble, you can tell me."

"I don't have time. I promise, I'll explain later. For now, I have to go," I tell him as I back away to the break room where my stuff is in a little locker.

He must sense the total freak-out I'm having because he lifts both hands like he's trying to calm me. "Okay, fine, but I need an explanation from you the next time you work. If you need anything, call me." He pulls the pen out from behind his ear and tears a little piece off a sheet of paper on the corkboard behind me and jots his number down. He rushes toward me and shoves the piece of paper at me.

"Thanks, Nick," I tell him, tucking the number down into my pocket. Without another word I slip into the break room and grab my purse and keys. Then I push through the door that leads out the back of the restaurant and hustle down to the dock so I can walk past the ice cream shop to wait for a while. I may just have to walk home and come back tomorrow to get my car. *Damn, I hate this. How did he find me here? I don't know anyone matching a description like the dude Nick described. It's not Lawson, but it's also not a description that matches anyone I remember serving, so it couldn't be a customer.*

After half an hour I slip through several parking lots of other businesses and restaurants and cross over Highway 19 onto Highway 44 and follow the sidewalk toward my neighborhood. I'm almost a block from where I have to turn when a truck startles me by pulling up on the sidewalk in front of me. I pause, already freaked out by the guy looking for me, my muscles in flight mode, ready to run when it dawns on me that it's Hudson's truck.

He jumps out of the driver's side and stalks back to me. The lights of oncoming traffic illuminate the anger etched into his features. For a second I stop, frozen with fear. That's the same expression my husband often would get right before he would beat the shit out of me. My mind tells me to turn and sprint the other way, but my feet don't listen. They're stuck in place, practically cemented to the ground.

"What in the hell are you doing walking around out here at night? This is a rough neighborhood," he growls at me. "Your car should be working fine after I changed the battery."

Finally, instinct kicks in and I step back from him, physically avoiding his anger, but still manage to answer defiantly. "I live here, remember?" I don't know where this give-it-right-back-to-him attitude comes from when he's near, but my fighting spirit flares up whenever he's present. My instinct may say run, but my mouth ends up arguing or hurling snotty remarks at him.

"You know what I mean. You have a car. Why aren't you driving it?"

"It's a long story. I'll have it back tomorrow. But none of that is your business. What are you doing here anyway?"

"I was out with friends and on my way home when I saw you, but that's not what's important here."

He turns like he's going back to his truck but before he can take a step away, he growls. Yes, actually growls out loud and spins back to face me. I notice his fists are clenched and it takes everything inside me not to take a few more steps away from the obviously angry man in front of me.

"Alright, get in," he says through clenched teeth. "I can't leave you walking on the side of the road over here. I'll end up reading about a woman either murdered or caught in a drive-by and then I'll feel guilty."

"That's stupid. I'm not your responsibility; you're being overly dramatic." Now my hand is on my hip and my eyes are narrowed on him.

"You can either get in the truck on your own or I'll put you inside myself. Either way, I'm not leaving you out here."

"Why do you care?" I ask, exasperated.

"That's the kind of guy I am. Now what's it going to be?"

I don't doubt he'll pick me up and put me in the truck, drawing more attention to us than he already has by pulling up on the sidewalk. *Ugh.* "Fine, I'll get in myself."

When we're both in the truck he pulls off the curb and heads toward my house. "You gonna tell me what's going on?"

His question pisses me off. "No, it shouldn't matter to you what's going on. I don't understand why you didn't just leave me on the side of the road. I'm not your problem. I'm a grown woman. I'm taking care of myself."

"Technically, you might be taking care of yourself, but you're doing a shitty job of it. Walking through this neighborhood at night is asking for any number of horrible things to happen to you." Hudson's jaw twitches like he's really pissed and he shakes his head.

"You don't need to worry about me. Just drop me off in front of my place and I'll be okay."

"How will you get back to your car tomorrow?"

I turn my head and glare at him. He knows that I'll walk.

"I guess I'll be by tomorrow to take you to your car. Is it working?"

"Yes, it's working fine," I huff, irritated that I have to answer to anyone.

"I can take you to get it now."

"No!" I say, a little too quickly and adamantly.

"You're leaving me with more questions than answers and I don't have a good feeling about any of it."

I remain quiet as he pulls down my street. When my place comes into view, my gut clenches. *Shit.* A skinny guy with a mullet hairstyle, wearing jeans and a dark T-shirt, matching the description Nick gave me, is walking around the outside of my place. His old beat-up black Camaro is parked out front. He must think that in a neighborhood like this no one will notice a strange person snooping around your house. The sad part about it is he's probably right. *Damn it!*

"Who's at your place?" Hudson asks as he slows down.

"I don't know, but can you keep driving?" Panic rises within me, making my voice almost squeaky as I slouch down in my seat so I can't be seen as we pass by. *I can't get out here. I don't know who that is, but it can't be good, considering my situation.* "Just don't stop!" I practically yell at him. The truck windows are tinted dark so it shouldn't be too obvious I'm in the vehicle, but I'm not taking any chances.

Hudson hits the gas and drives out of my neighborhood quickly and then north on Highway 19 toward the power plant. The white smoke rising in a single pillar up ahead can be seen even in the dark as the buildings and houses become sparser the farther down the road we drive.

"Where are we going? I just asked you to get past my house, not drop me off in the boondocks."

"I've got a house in the north part of Crystal River off of 581. No one comes down my road and very few people know it exists. You'll be safe there while you fill me in on what's going on. I've known something was off with you since I laid eyes on you that first night outside the trailer."

"I don't even know you. By this time tomorrow I could be chopped up into a hundred pieces and fed to the alligators if I go out there with you."

He finishes an epic eye roll with a look that tells me he thinks I'm an idiot. "If I wanted to hurt you, I could've done it a while ago. Seriously, think about it. I've seen you several times. I know where you live and where you work, so it wouldn't be hard. Every time I see you, I try to help you in some way. Why waste all that time and effort if I just want to cut you up into little pieces?"

"Fine," I huff. "I honestly don't have any choice at this point."

We ride the rest of the way in silence. He's right; this place is in the middle of nowhere and I doubt anyone but him and whoever built this place has ever been here. We pass through an open gate down a dirt road flanked by overgrown weeds. When we finally reach a small clearing, a little, gray blockhouse comes into view. To the left, about 200 yards past the house is a pond with cattails lining most of the edges, and by the murky looks of it, it is a breeding ground for gators and snakes. I shiver at the thought. The house is the plainest I've ever seen. No flair, no ornamentation, no landscaping, no personality... nothing. It looks like it was built in the last 20 years, though, and is in good shape, so it's nothing to complain about. It's just nothing to brag about either.

After unlocking the front door he leads me inside and I find the interior to be as utilitarian as the outside. No frills, no personal touches of any sort. Just a couch, a television, a beat-up coffee table, a floor lamp, a ceiling fan and nothing else. There's a small galley kitchen off the back of the living area and a short hallway that I assume leads to a bedroom or two and a bathroom. It's clean, but I can't get over the lack of personality this place has. My rental has more pizzazz and heart than this place and it's a shithole of an apartment.

"Have a seat. You want a drink?" he asks.

"Yeah, I think I do."

"I have beer or water."

"Whiskey would be better, but beer will work." I need something with a bite to it. I'm tired and cranky and I have no idea what I'm going to do.

He pops the top on a bottle of Coors Light and passes it to me before sitting on the arm of the couch and looking down at me. His eyes are assessing and the longer he stares the more I squirm. "So, what's the story?"

"Are you sure you even want to know? It's not that big of a deal. I've made it on my own this far."

Crossing his arms over his barrel chest he answers me. "I'm certain I want to hear it."

*Damn. Okay, fine.* "My husband used to beat me and the last time he did, it was bad enough to put me in the hospital. I decided I was done living that way so I filed a report with the police and then filed for divorce. He was arrested before I was released from the hospital and posted bail right after I was discharged. I knew if he found me he'd kill me, so I packed up my crap and left. My parents are dead and Lawson made sure I didn't have any friends left, so I've been alone, on the run, for about six months now."

"I'm assuming the guy outside my house is someone he hired to find me since I've never seen him before in my life. He showed up at the Lobster Lounge toward the end of my shift, asking for me. I asked Nick, the bartender, to stall so I could get out of there. I was afraid someone might be waiting for me at my car so I decided to walk home the back way. At this point, walking through the worst part of town with the possibility that something would happen seemed like a better idea than facing some guy who is probably there to drag me back to Lawson."

"So your ex beat you up and you got tired of it and left? Now he's looking for you," he quickly summarizes every muscle in his body suddenly tense.

"Yes," I confirm and take a long drink of my beer. "He's also on the run. The cops are looking for him, but at my last check-in they hadn't found him."

He stands and pulls out his wallet, producing a card that he then hands to me.

*Hudson McCormick* and *Sunset Security* are the first two things I see.

"You have a security agency?"

"Yes. Mike, the guy I was at dinner with the other night, and I just opened it up a few months ago. We worked together at Security Six in Tampa, but neither one of us was happy living down there so we decided to relocate and start our own."

"Is there enough business here to keep you busy?" *This is a sleepy little town; I can't imagine their services being needed here.*

"No, but we knew that coming up here and neither of us minds traveling, which we will do more as the business builds. Our home base is here because when it's time to wind down and take a break we want peace and quiet. Both are plentiful here. That being said, I don't have a job I'm working right now and I can help you."

"You don't even know me, and what little you do know makes me think you *really* don't like me. Besides that, I honestly can't afford you right now. I'm sure your services don't come cheap and I'm on a limited budget because I can't access any of my accounts."

"I don't know you enough to like or not like you. What I

don't like is people makin' stupid choices that could get them hurt. Now that I know your story, I get why you've made the choices you have. It explains a lot. I don't need to get paid for this job; I'm doing okay. Besides, I can't lay my head on my pillow at night and actually get sleep knowing you might not be safe. It's not right. Not when I have the means to do something about it."

"Just my luck I'd run into a Boy Scout along the way," I grumble.

"Furthest thing from a Boy Scout you're ever gonna meet, babe."

I look over to find him smirking at me in an annoyingly handsome way that I shouldn't even be noticing in my situation. I lean back against the couch, resting my head, and look at his ceiling. The beer bottle, half empty now, is resting in my hand on my thigh as I contemplate what to do.

---

5

---

## Hudson

---

This is a pretty jacked-up situation. It's interesting that of all the people in this town to take notice of her, it's me. Of course, I do have a soft spot for pretty women with curly hair. Always have. Doesn't matter if it is black, brown, red or blond. Something about a woman with wild hair does it for me.

I need to get a handle on her ex, though, and the only way to do that is to look into the guy.

Stacey is still staring at the ceiling like it's the most interesting thing she's ever seen. I know she's overwhelmed and probably scared, even though she puts on a good tough-girl act, but finessing any situation is not my strong suit. When it comes to dealing with clients, that part is Mike's job. He's straightforward but still has a natural charm that settles people. Me, I tend to piss them off by stating the obvious too abruptly. I come from a family of outspoken, sarcastic folks. It's not in my DNA to smooth things out.

I can't sit here and wait for her to come to terms with this whole thing if I'm going to get her out of my house soon. Which I need to do for my own personal sanity. The sweet brown doe eyes, the curly brown hair and the sass she throws my way are more than I can deal with long term. *Guess I need to get this show on the road.*

"To make this easier, I need all the information you can give me on your ex."

She turns to face me, her head still resting on the back of the couch. "If I had another option, I'd use it, but I think I'm out of those. What do you want to know?" Her mood is more mellow, almost resigned, and I wonder what kind of talk she just had with herself to settle down that much.

"Hold on." I go back to my room and grab a notepad sitting on top of one of the boxes. I'm notorious for making notes and lists on paper for everything, so I always have one around. As I return to the living room I peel back the pages until I reach a blank sheet and say, "Anything you can think of. Start with the basics."

"Lawson Allen. Thirty-two years old. No brothers or sisters. Father and mother live in Charleston, South Carolina, where he grew up. When he turned 25, he got access to his trust fund. His family had a commercial fishing business for over 100 years and sold out to a corporation for a crazy amount of money. His grandfather set it all up in trust for the kids and grandkids, so Lawson quit his job at an investment firm after putting in two years right after college. I met him when he was working at the investment firm."

"What does he do all day if he doesn't work?"

"Apparently, half the women in town, behind my back. He plays golf at the country club and he drinks…a lot."

"Sounds like a gem," I reply dryly.

"He was great until I caught him screwing around on me the first time. When I called him out on it, he shut me up with his fists, which hurt like hell, but it could be hidden by clothing. Within a month of that incident the beatings were a regular part of my life. My friends knew something was up. I went from being an outgoing, active young woman to nervous and quiet in a heartbeat. You couldn't slam a door near me or accidentally drop something on the ground without me losing my shit. My best friend from college confronted me several times and I denied it every time."

"Why?"

"I was embarrassed and afraid. Lawson's crazy and I didn't put it past him to go after my friends to hurt me more. He has the kind of money that can cover a multitude of sins and he apparently knows people to help him out with that stuff. He plays a poker game once a month down in Savannah with some very scary men, and I didn't want to end up on their radar either."

"Seems like there's more to this than him just wanting to keep you around as a punching bag." I phrase it as a statement but leave it hanging like a question. *She's not telling me something. A man doesn't go from being careful where he places his fists to putting her in the hospital without a reason to lose his shit that bad.*

She shifts her eyes back to the ceiling and doesn't give me any more.

"Why did you end up in the hospital?"

"I told you—he's a vicious son of a bitch."

"Doesn't answer my question. He went from putting marks on you that could be hidden, to sending you to the hospital."

"Long story, but basically he thought I was about to run away and went nuts. He thought he killed me, so he freaked and left the house. My neighbor found me when she came over that afternoon. She called 9-1-1. Can we not talk about this part?" she asks, and I can hear the tears in her voice.

I hate when women cry. "Yeah, this should get me started. I'm sure I'll have more questions, but for now, this is good. I'm sure you know this already, but if he's found you, you can't go back to work."

She closes her eyes and her lip trembles a little. "Yeah, I figured. He always finds a way to take all the things I enjoy away. Can you pull Mr. Clark, the owner, aside at the Lounge and let him know that I'm sorry? He knew a little about my situation and was helping me. I hate to leave him without coverage on my shifts."

"You liked working at the Lobster Lounge?" I scoff, not concealing my disbelief.

"I've always enjoyed a hard day of work, and I like being around people. Nick, the bartender, is funny and some of the waitresses are sweet. It's a good job."

I didn't expect that from her, so I have no idea what to say. If she's been living high on the hog with her ex for a few years, I'm surprised she even wants to work at all, much less take orders and deal with asshole tourists and entitled locals.

"The internet is shit out here. I need to head to my office and look into some of this. I don't have cable out here yet, but sometimes I can get a few channels; I'm sorry about that. You're safe though. Lock up, just in case. I'll add my number to your phone. You can crash in my bed and get some sleep, and if you need me, call."

"Why are you doing this for me?"

"It's just what I do."

Stacey mutters something about me being vague and I'd like to say, 'back at you,' but decide against it. It's been a long day and I can tell she's worn out.

"I changed the sheets this morning so they're clean. Pillows might be a little lumpy, but they'll do in a pinch. My bedroom is the one on the right. There is a bathroom in there. Towels and washcloths are on the shelf. Use what you need. Make yourself at home. I'll text you when I'm coming back so I don't freak you out. If anyone else shows up, dial 9-1-1 and get in the back of my closet. No one is supposed to be out here and only a few people even know this place exists."

"Thank you… for everything," she says quietly as she stands and shuffles down the short hallway to my room. Her thick, curly brown ponytail is the last thing I see before she disappears.

I don't know what to do with her. One minute she's giving me attitude and the next she's quiet and withdrawn. I definitely like the attitude better than the withdrawn, but I don't need to be concerned with either. What I do need is to help her get out of this situation and be done with it. My mind is muddled, leaving me agitated as I drive away from my house. I turn out onto Highway 19 and head toward the office.

Our office is the middle unit in a row of old, unique office buildings on Citrus Avenue in the heart of Crystal River. On one side of us there's a lawyer and on the other is an Irish Pub. At this time of night both are closed and the area is a ghost town, so I'm surprised when I pull up to the parking space directly in front of the building and see Mike's truck sitting there too. The light's on inside. *What the hell is he doing here? I thought he was going home to talk to Summer on the phone before he called it a night.*

The small office that we moved into a few weeks ago has a tiny reception area with a mahogany desk where our receptionist will soon sit. Past that is a short hallway with an office on the left, which is mine, and an office on the right, which is Mike's. The walls are still white and blank, much like my own house.

I use the key to open the door. Mike sticks his head out of his office door and asks, "What the hell are you doing here?"

"I could ask you the same."

"I couldn't sleep. Computer at our place is shit and I've been house-hunting, so I thought I'd do it here. Summer was too tired from a long shoot today to talk long. I don't think she realized how tired she would be now that she's pregnant. I should have gone with her instead of Thomas. I trust Thomas, but—"

Thomas is Mike's younger brother who recently joined us

here at Sunset Security. He's retired Army and as tough as they come. Summer had a crazy stalker last year and now has it written into her contract for personal security, but we were in the transition phase of getting this office going so he sent Thomas with her. "I get it. You'd feel better if you were there to take care of her at the end of the day, not just play body-guard. Why don't you go down there now? She's only got a week left. I can hold the fort down here. It's not like we have a stampede of clients beating the door down yet."

"Summer and I talked about it and she really wants me to get this business going and keep looking for a permanent house."

"Why are you house-hunting when you just got into your rental?"

"We really want to be settled into a place and not have to worry about moving while dealing with a baby."

"Just relax, man. When it comes time to move, Thomas and I will help, and you know your parents will come up here too. Don't rush buying a house when your rental is freaking awesome and perfect for right now. Now back to Summer—"

"I really think she's saying no because she doesn't want to put me out, and I'm trying to not be a Neanderthal and over-ride her request just because it will make me feel better."

"I understand, and she's safe with your brother for now. It'll be okay. Just hang in there."

"Okay, so now you know all of my shit. Why are you here at this hour?" He lifts an eyebrow and tilts his head, waiting for my answer.

"Remember the waitress at the Lobster Lounge? The new one."

"Yeah. Pretty, young, brown curly hair, great smile."

"That's the one," I confirm.

"What about her?"

"She's in trouble. I found her walking near Eighth Avenue

tonight. She's living there. Apparently, her ex is a nasty piece of work and she's been running from him for a while. Seems like he found her."

"Let me guess, you took her to your *Friday the 13th* style cabin in the boondocks and are keeping her safe."

My eyes narrow on him because I'm not *that* predictable.

"Don't give me that look. You're not the kind of guy to find out a woman needs help and leave her on the side of the road. Oh, and let's not forget, she *is* your type." Mike grins.

I ignore his little chuckle and fill him in on the whole story. "I figure while she's sleeping, I can do some digging and maybe track him down to see if he's here."

"Want me to pull his financials?"

"Nah, you keep house-hunting. If I run into a snag, I'll let you know. I won't be able to sleep, so going back there isn't much of an option."

"Okay, just let me know if you want me to jump in."

"Thanks, man."

———

BY FOUR IN the morning my eyes are blurring, but I have a much better idea of what kind of man Lawson Allen is and I like him less than when I heard he was a wife-beating asshole. He's a slippery son of a bitch. I have no doubt that he's hired the mullet guy to find her. If I can figure out who he is, that will help. I doubt the ex will show up until mullet guy gets his hands on her, though. He seems to be laying low, probably because he's on the run from the cops. I'm going to call a buddy of mine from the Navy and ask him to do some digging. He lives outside of Charleston. In the meantime, I'll keep her out of sight.

When I let myself into the house, the hum of the old refrigerator in the kitchen is the only thing that breaks the silence. I kick my work boots off by the front door and set my keys on the kitchen counter. Then I move quietly through the house to check on Stacey.

She's curled up under the covers, softly snoring. Her wild hair is coming out of her messy ponytail and curling in little wisps around her cheeks and forehead. Her face is relaxed and sweet in sleep, all the little worry lines are smooth and nonexistent. *How could any man hit a woman, much less one this delicate and beautiful?* After dealing with Carmen for so long I can understand being driven to the brink of insanity, but to actually lift a hand to her…never. If Lawson doesn't show up here in Crystal River, I'll go looking for him and give him a taste of what he gave her.

I stand there watching her a little too long and finally turn and move to the couch. Grabbing my shirt by the collar I tug it over my head and lay it across the back of the couch. Then I lie down and angle myself so I can fit on the cushions. Luckily, I learned how to sleep anywhere, anytime, when I was in the Navy, or I'd be screwed. My body, especially my shoulders and thighs, are so much bigger than what is meant to fit on this couch. I could have put her out here, but I wanted her to have some level of comfort. That bed isn't one you'd find at the Ritz, but it's probably better than what she's been sleeping on at her place.

I close my eyes and force Stacey out of my brain long enough to fall asleep.

—————

THE NEXT MORNING I wake to find Stacey quietly stretching on the floor by the wall with her legs straight in front of her, her fingers touching her toes. When I shift my body a little, she looks over to me. "Morning," she says quietly.

"Morning." I sit up and stretch my arms above my head to help get the blood flowing.

"Sorry if I woke you. There wasn't enough room in your bedroom to stretch and I've been awake for a little while. My joints were hurting so I had to move around."

"What time is it?" I ask, hoping I didn't sleep too late.

"Eight."

"Damn, I never sleep that late anymore."

"I figured you were out late, so I left you alone."

"I was, but I'm used to functioning on a little bit of sleep."

I rub my face and sit back against the couch. "Everything I found on Lawson last night makes me think he spent some good money on the guy who found you yesterday. I doubt your husband is here, though. Doesn't seem to be the type to get his hands dirty until it's absolutely necessary. My guess is that he won't be far from here. We need to keep you out of sight until I figure out who the dude with the mullet is. This morning I'll run to the store to get anything you might need. I'm sure you've figured out I don't really do anything but sleep here."

"Yeah, the only thing I found in there," she jerks her head toward the kitchen, "was a half-empty gallon of whole milk." She wrinkles her nose like that's gross.

"That's the only thing I drink besides water and beer. When I go out, I'll also drop by your apartment to get anything you want from there."

Stacey's gaze has shifted from mine to the floor. It takes a moment before she finally looks me in the eye again. This time a sadness takes over, seeming to weigh her shoulders down a little. "I'm a prisoner all over again. He's not beating me to keep me in line. Instead, he's tracking me like prey. I don't think I'll ever be free again."

Her words cause an ache in my chest, right behind my sternum. I want to soothe her and help her understand I'll do what I can to help her, even if this is the last thing I want to be doing, but I don't think she'd believe me at this point. I've been such a dick to her so far and she doesn't deserve that.

Pulling her knees up to her chest and wrapping her arms around them like she's protecting herself, she says, "I know this is a lot to ask since I'm already dragging you into this and staying in your house," she glances around, clearly not impressed with my little house, "but I'd like to have Screamer with me."

"Screamer?" I ask as I tilt my head, trying to figure out who Screamer is.

"My cat. The one I was rescuing the night I met you at the crack trailer."

I groan. "Babe—I hate cats." I mean, I really hate them. I've always been a dog person. The only reason I don't have one now is because I'm out of town so much. I don't want to try to find someone to watch the beast every time I leave. That's a huge pain in the ass for Mike and Summer with their roly-poly basset hound.

"I realize it's a lot to ask, but she's all I have. I can buy more clothes, get a new computer and shoes, but I can't replace her. Please?" Her voice is soft, close to defeated, and I hate it. I liked it better when she was defiant and grouchy.

"I'll go by there and if she's around I'll grab her. She better not scratch me up or she'll be in the bed of my truck on the way here, though."

Her smile is instantaneous and bright, worth it to drive a damn cat to my house.

"What else do you want from your place?"

"I don't have much. Whatever you can grab. My laptop computer, clothes, backpack, toiletries in the bathroom. What's in there is mine. It won't take you long. Also, go into the closet in the bedroom and peel back the carpet on the left side of the closet floor, pull up the floorboard and grab the grocery bag in there."

"Got it. What does this cat look like? I only saw eyes in the dark last time. I don't want to nab someone else's cat."

"Screamer's a calico."

I give her a blank look because I have no idea what that means.

"She has a white belly with a black patch over one eye and an orange patch over the other. The fur on her back is orange and black. Her eyes are green and her nose is pink with black at the bottom. There aren't any others in the neighborhood like her. The others are all black or gray, so you won't mistake her. She'll also likely be the one prancing around like she's too good to give you the time of day. Take a Slim Jim strip of jerky with you and break it up. She'll come straight to you."

"Your cat eats Slim Jims?"

"Slim Jims rock! Why wouldn't she?"

"Never heard of that before."

"I didn't have any cat food when she showed up at my place, so I had to improvise and that's what she liked most. It's how we became friends."

Stacey chews on her bottom lip for a second before she asks, "How big is your property?"

"About 10 acres. Why?"

"Can I at least walk around the property? I can't stay cooped up in here all day. I'll go nuts. After being trapped with Lawson for so long it gives me hives to think about looking at the walls for hours on end."

"You can, but you need to be careful. The wildlife out here tends to be…wild."

She cocks her head and waits for me to elaborate.

"Panthers, bears, gators, snakes, coyotes, deer, fox, and I feel like I'm leaving something out, but you get the picture. If I were you, I'd hang tight and wait for me to come back. I'll be glad to walk you around the property when I return."

"Well, do you have anything I can read? Until you bring

my stuff back, I don't have a damn thing to do and I'm not the kind of woman to sit on my ass all day."

"I may have a technical manual you could dig into." I shrug, feeling bad because I know she's going to go stir-crazy. "I'll get back here as soon as I can. It would just suck for you to survive your husband only to get eaten by a coyote out here."

"Fine," she huffs as she plops on my couch after I stand up, with a serious pout to her pretty lips.

*I need to get this situation under control and get her out of my house. I can already tell she's going to be trouble for me, and that doesn't include the issue with her ex.*

# 6

## Stacey

This is freaking torture! Absolute torture! I hate sitting still on a good day. I can usually handle chilling out for a short period of time if there is a good movie on or an old sitcom I like, and especially if I have a good book. I have none of the above so I'm going batty. If I didn't have a healthy fear of snakes and alligators, I would head out that door and ignore the threat of bears or panthers.

Since he left me here alone with nothing to do, I guess I'll have a look around inside. I've always had an elevated level of curiosity. If you had asked my Aunt Leona when she was alive, she'd have said it's a wonder that my curiosity didn't get me in more trouble, because it always led me somewhere I wasn't supposed to be. I can't help it. I don't like unanswered questions and I always have a ton of those.

Hudson's bedroom is my starting point. Opening drawers and peeking inside, I don't find much other than cargo pants, T-shirts, long-sleeved shirts, hats, socks and underwear. Disappointed, but not deterred, I open the closet door only to find one suit hanging up, a couple of shirts, combat boots and one pair of leather flip-flops on the floor. *There's not anything remotely interesting here.* I push an olive green canvas duffel bag out of the way, hoping for a trap door or something even halfway exciting, and find nothing.

Frustrated and bored, I yank the bag back into place and something tumbles out. I reach down to grab it, realizing it's a picture. I stand and hold it up to get a better view. *Damn.* It's a seriously handsome Hudson in his dress whites uniform, standing next to a woman in a tight-fitting, knee-length white lace dress. By the veil on her head and small red bouquet in her hand, it's obvious I'm looking at a wedding photo. *Hudson's married?*

I look more closely and study the woman. There's something very familiar about her. She's beautiful, a little more makeup than I ever wear, but still pretty. Slender, but built in the boobs department. She's smiling at the camera and Hudson is smiling at her.

The longer I stare, the more I believe I've seen her before. *But where? Maybe she came into the Lobster Lounge. I didn't notice a ring on his finger and this place obviously isn't hiding a wife.* Something about this guy tells me he has no idea how to physically harm a woman. His words, though, can cut like a knife, but I don't think he would ever raise a hand to a woman.

I shove the picture back under the bag, close the closet door and return to the couch. Once I'm sprawled out with my feet up on the arm, I stare at the ceiling, wondering how I'm going to pass the time. I must doze off because I'm awakened when the door shuts with a thump. I shoot up to a sitting position with a gasp and turn toward the noise. Hudson is paused inside the door, obviously understanding that he spooked me.

"You okay?" his deep voice rumbles, but he doesn't move.

"Um, yeah. I must have dozed off. You startled me. What time is it?"

"About two o'clock."

"Damn, that was a long nap. I never nap."

"You must have needed it, then."

"Or I was bored straight to sleep," I mumble bitchily. Then I realize he's back but doesn't have my cat in his arms. A tremor of panic runs through me and I tense. "Where's Screamer?"

"Truck."

"She's out in the truck? She's going to melt out there."

"Babe—I left the air conditioner running. That cat is a pain in the ass. You get to drag her out of the vehicle. I'm done. I had to chase her to catch her and then she screamed the whole way here. If you let her loose out here on my property to get eaten, I won't cry about it."

"Don't be mean," I chastise him as I brush past him and out the door to grab my traumatized cat. I can hear her crying as soon as I step out the front door and he's right, it's annoying. I can't say I'd be happy about listening to that all the way out here either, but I'm not about to admit it to him. I open the passenger door and see my stuff piled all over the back seat. Screamer is lodged in the corner with her head sticking out of a folded-up blanket.

"Screamer, honey, I'm so sorry."

A nasty howling response comes from the poor cat.

Behind me, Hudson suggests, "Let me get some of your stuff out of the way so you can climb up there and pull her out. Although, I have to tell you, if she keeps that up inside, I won't have a problem letting her out to explore."

I turn and glare at him before I step out of the way and let him get to my things. He's kind of an ass. I can't figure out why someone who seems so put out to have us here has gone to all this trouble.

When he steps out of the way with an armload of stuff and heads to the front door, I climb up into the truck and reach out to pet the unhappy fuzz ball. "Come on, Screamer, girl. Settle down. It's only for a day or two. At least here you'll get something to eat."

The howling stops once I find the perfect spot behind her left ear. After a minute of this, I scoop her up and hold her close to me. Her loud meow startles me as I move past Hudson through the front door. It's almost as if she had to have one final word with him before she was done. I sit on the couch and scratch behind her ear again. Once Hudson is inside with the last of my stuff, I loosen my hold on her body and she jumps down, sprinting through the little house. After disappearing into Hudson's room, the house falls silent.

"That cat better not crap in my room."

"Don't worry, she's housebroken. She's just hiding for a bit until she gets the courage to explore. Thank you. I know it was a pain in the ass, but I feel better having her here."

He nods once and looks over at my stuff. "You can use the dresser and closet in the spare room. Let me move a couple of things. No bed in there, though, so you'll have to stay in my bed for now. Hopefully, we'll have this resolved in a few days and you can go back to South Carolina. I'm hoping you never have to return to that shithole apartment on Eighth Avenue again."

I lift my chin. "I'm not leaving this town."

"What?" he asks, clearly confused.

"Once I'm done running for my life, I'll stay in Crystal River. I'll just find a nicer place to live than Eighth Avenue. I love it here."

A strange expression passes over his face. "You're staying?"

"That's what I said," my tone a little sassy. I have no idea why I'm not afraid to get a little mouthy, considering he's the same size as my crazy ex who liked to beat on me, but I can't seem to help the smart-ass comments that fly out of my mouth when I talk to him. Maybe it's just that after all this time of holding it in, I can't bottle it up anymore.

He shakes his head and returns to his room, shutting the door behind him. I take my stuff into the second bedroom, which is set up like an office with an extra dresser, and unpack so it will be out of the way.

As I'm bent over, pushing the bottom drawer closed, he pauses in the doorway. "Put on some shorts and sneakers and I'll show you around the property."

"Okay." Even though I feel bad about leaving Screamer to adjust on her own, I can't pass up the opportunity to get out of this house and take in some fresh air. I shut the door to the office and pull on a pair of running shorts and an old T-shirt. Then I tug on socks and my running shoes. I open the door and return to the living room where Hudson is standing, waiting. His eyes start at my sneakers and travel up my legs, over my hips and breasts, to my face. It probably happens quickly but it feels like a long slow stroke with his eyes, my skin heating along with the upward sweep. When our eyes meet, I probably blush 15 shades of pink before I turn toward the door, because if I'm not mistaken, he liked what he saw and it made me feel warmer than it should have.

He doesn't seem to care for me very much so I can't understand why he'd look me over like I'm the finest steak he's ever seen. *Probably just a natural male response.* He's a good-looking guy so I imagine he doesn't have a problem getting female attention. However, he lives in a serial-killer house in the middle of nowhere, so maybe that deters some who might be willing to come home with him.

He doesn't remark about my clothing but instead opens the door and walks through it. I hurry behind him, shutting the door.

Once I pass him he turns around, locks the door and shoves his keys in his pocket. "Let's go."

About 50-feet from the back of his house, the grass changes

from short and well-kept to overgrown and wild. It makes my legs itch as we move at a medium pace.

As we're rounding the pond, movement out of the corner of my eye draws my attention. A four-foot alligator runs from the bank, pushing off into the water and disappearing in the murky depths. I, of course, jump and run forward like I need to get away. I've never seen an alligator in the wild, only at zoos and on television.

"Stacey, stop," Hudson's command is short and blunt, halting me in my tracks.

"Did you see that?" I ask almost hysterically, while starting to move again.

"Yeah, you scared him. He was probably enjoying some time in the sun until we spooked him. Relax. I have my hunting knife." He lifts his shirt up and I see the handle and holster of a very large knife at his waist. "Stay close to me. I know the areas to avoid and I can handle it if something comes for us."

"Comes for us?" my voice goes high and squeaky.

"Well, it's unlikely, but still possible."

"How often do you come back here? It looks…primitive." I glance around, trying to find evidence of a worn-down footpath or anything that points to him coming out here.

"Several times a week. I love it out here. It's peaceful."

We approach a thicket of bushes and trees and fear slides around in my belly. After seeing that alligator so close to the house, I'm not feeling like running into that condensed area.

"Come on, I'm gonna lead the way. Stay close and stay directly behind me. Once we get past this part, we'll make it to Gator Creek."

"Um, I wasn't crazy about the one gator we just saw, I'm not sure I want to find a whole creek full of them."

"They aren't usually this far up in the creek. They stay

closer to the pond. I wouldn't take you there if I didn't think you'd like it. Come on."

He holds out a hand and I hesitate before I finally take it. He places my hand on his hip. "Follow me. Stay close."

"Okay," I answer, still not sure about this, but gripping his belt loops with my fingers nonetheless.

We weave in and out of small oak trees, tall pine trees, overgrown bushes and vines until we finally make it through to a clearing. Spanish moss hangs down from several large, old oak trees, giving them a majestic, timeless beauty that I didn't expect to find out here. The cicadas are loud out here, even with us tromping through the brush. An earthy scent fills the air and I know we are close to water. A squirrel scampers across a branch and disappears on the back side of the smallest of the huge oaks.

"This place is beautiful," I whisper for no reason other than I'm in awe.

"Yeah," he glances back at me with a smile, "but you haven't seen the best part yet. Come on."

This time he grabs my hand and pulls me next to him as we make our way across the clearing to the big trees. The closer we get, the louder the trickle of water becomes. Hudson pauses and glances in the branches of the two trees we're about to walk under and I shudder to think of what he could be looking for. He must feel it because he asks, "You okay?"

"Yeah, just got a little nervous when I saw you scanning the trees for some reason."

"Snakes. They like to hang out in the trees sometimes."

"Snakes!" I practically shriek.

"Calm down, there weren't any up there."

"Snakes in the trees?" I can't calm down. I hate snakes. Don't like the look of them, even the harmless ones, don't like the hissing sound they make, I don't like a single thing about them.

"Didn't you ever play outside as a kid or did you live in the big city?" His tone is slightly condescending and it irritates me.

"Yes, I played outside. As a matter of fact, I grew up in the South and spent all of my days running around barefooted down the dirt road. I'm not sure what kind of opinion you have of me, but I wasn't raised a priss."

"Your reaction to the critters around here says different."

"We didn't have snakes and gators in the trailer park. We had stray cats, pit bulls chained to trees, chickens wandering aimlessly, and drunken, middle-aged male predators."

There is a long pause as he studies me, a weird expression passing over his face before he wipes it clean and says, "Little different, but no less scary. I won't let anything happen to you, so relax." He squeezes my hand and tugs me along.

As soon as we pass the trunk of the first tree, the creek comes into sight. The water is trickling over a bunch of rocks and moving down further until it disappears around the bend. There's not enough of it here to submerge yourself but enough to wade probably up to your knees. The giant oak branches along the banks drape gracefully, leaving the creek shrouded in shade. It almost looks like a lost world here, nothing like the rest of his property. *This might be my new favorite place, minus the wildlife.*

Without even thinking, I release his hand and take a seat near the water's edge on a large stone. I remove my socks and shoes and dip my feet in, relishing the cold water.

"I can't believe it's so cold!" I squeak.

"Only because it's spring-fed about a hundred feet that way." He points upstream to an area covered in heavy brush.

"If you follow it down past my property line it comes out on the old Baird property. Paxton and Shay live out there. Good people, but private. There is an area near their house that's deep enough to actually submerge in without rolling in the mud. I could dam it up here and do the same, but I like it the way it is."

"Me too," I tell him softly. Something like this is a natural gift; you don't mess with it, you just enjoy it for what it is.

He moves to the rock next to mine and sits down, removing his shoes and socks, following my lead by sinking his toes in the water. After a few minutes of peace, just relaxing, he clears his throat. "You lived in a trailer park?"

I shift uncomfortably and answer. I hate talking about it. Lawson taught me to be ashamed of it. "Yeah, you didn't find that out when you were looking into Lawson?"

"Didn't check on you. Should have, but didn't. Once I found the first couple of pieces of info on him, I dove in. Why don't you just tell me so I don't have to waste my time?"

"Mama died of cancer when I was eight years old. Daddy followed in a car accident two years later. I was already spending most of my time with my great-aunt Leona in the trailer park, so the social worker just helped to make it permanent." I sigh, wondering how different my life would be if I had been put into foster care instead of at Aunt Leona's.

"So, how did you meet a man like Lawson?" His voice is quieter this time and I wonder what changed.

"I got a full scholarship to the University of South Carolina, graduated and got a job at Ruckerheimer Investment Firm out of Charlotte, North Carolina. He worked there too, but I didn't know him. About six months into the job our paths crossed in the elevator. He asked me out the following week and we dated about a year before we got married. Six months after we married, he got his trust fund, quit his job, convinced me to quit and moved us to Charleston. Once we got to Charleston, he forbade me to get a job, insisting that I needed to learn to relax and live a little. After that, he found ways to isolate me. My friends from college fell by the wayside and he wouldn't allow me do anything with his friends' wives without him there. By the time the beatings began, I was trapped with no way out. The rest is history."

"Small dick," he mutters.

Stunned by his words, I turn to him. "What?"

"Only men with small dicks do that to a woman."

I bust out laughing because it's true. He wasn't well-endowed and I honestly didn't know what to do with it. He got my attention because he was handsome, confident and gave me a level of attention I had only dreamed of getting from another human being at that point. The life I lived up until meeting him made him look like a hot fudge sundae on a sultry July day. By the time I figured out that he was the worst kind of brain freeze I could imagine, I was trapped.

"I'm guessing by the laughin' that it's true," he notes with a boyish grin.

That comment only makes me laugh harder. He smiles a full white-toothed smile for the first time since I met him and it stops me completely. *Holy hell. When he's not smiling, I get the visual of a smoldering fire. Hot enough to melt your skin, but the full effect of the flames is missing. But when that smile surfaces, damn, the heat in the vicinity jumps up 100 degrees and will set any woman, and some men, in the area on fire in an instant.*

My expression must reflect my feelings because his laugh dies instantly and his focus shifts from my eyes to my mouth. Little tingles tiptoe down my spine and my breath catches. Earlier, I wanted to be mad at him; after all, he hasn't been very friendly to me. But something changed just now between us. I have no idea what, but I just know the air is suddenly supercharged with a heat and electricity I've never felt from another human being before. Some kind of invisible magnetic force is pulling us together. My stomach tightens and my toes curl against the sandy creek floor, and our mouths are now mere inches apart. So close I can feel his breath ghost across my lips. My heart races and my hands become clammy. My mind falls in a wicked haze where the only thing I can see is Hudson and the only thing I want are his lips pressed to mine. This is a bad idea, but my body is coming alive like it hasn't in years, maybe ever. Heat is spreading to my core, my breasts are growing heavy and the desire to close the distance is too strong to resist. *How did I end up in this situation?*

# 7

# Hudson

When has the prelude to a kiss ever been this potent? It's taken my usually focused brain and caused it to jumble. All I can see is her mouth. All I can think about is tasting her and what could come after that. The thought of throwing her down out here in the middle of my favorite spot and taking her with my mouth, my hands and my cock is completely overwhelming. So, even though I know it's a horrible idea, I'm not going to stop myself from getting that taste of her. I'm finally close enough that when her tongue sneaks out to wet her own lips it touches mine and I bridge the distance. My mouth presses against hers and instead of a soft, slow kiss like she deserves, I delve in, my tongue connecting with hers, taking what I need. *Damn, if it isn't better than I expected.* Her hands grip my shoulders, nails digging into the tight flesh. She lights up like a Roman candle. Bright, hot and beautiful at one single touch.

It's been too long since a woman and a kiss affected me like this. In this moment, I need to stay connected to her more than I need to breathe. My muscles flex as I prepare to lift her and take her to a soft spot in the grass to continue this when a crash in the woods across the creek has us jerking back from one anther like we were splashed with icy water. Her eyes are wide and fearful as they swing toward the area where the noise is coming from. "What was that?" she asks in a breathy whisper.

Another crash of brush and she's up on her feet, scrambling to grab her socks and shoes. The small trees about 50 yards out flatten and the loud snuffle sound of an animal breaks through the sound of the cicadas.

"Shoes on. Time to go," I order, but I didn't need to because she's shoving her feet in her sneakers and clumsily hopping back the way we came. Once her foot is pressed into the shoe, she's on the run. It only takes a second to catch her once I have my shoes on too.

"Oh my God! What the hell is that?" she demands to know, huffing and puffing as she runs.

"A bear, so don't stop till we get to the pond."

"A what?!" she shrieks and runs faster. I'm actually surprised by her speed. She's faster than a jackrabbit on the run. I glance behind us and don't see anything. We were probably out of there before the bear even thought to follow. Once we reach the edge of the pond, I slow to a walk, putting my hands on my head to catch my breath.

"Didn't know you were a runner," I say.

"Told you I got a full scholarship to college."

"I assumed it was for academics."

"Nope. Distance runner. I never stopped doing it, I just hid it so Lawson wouldn't know that I'd be able to run from him eventually."

We're quiet the rest of the way. My mind rolls around the regret and the irritation at my lack of control. *I shouldn't have kissed her. Damn, it was good, but it was wrong and I know better.* Even though her reaction proved that she wanted it too, I know to keep my hands off of clients. They're vulnerable and too easy to take advantage of.

Stacey probably thinks I'm an asshole for making a move in

the middle of her life crisis. After that, I would agree. *Why would I do that when I don't want anything to do with any woman long-term after dealing with Carmen for the last five years? Besides, you don't just mess around with a woman like Stacey. She deserves better and should've had it all along. She's the kind you spend the rest of your life busting your balls to make hers better.*

When we enter the house, I go to the kitchen and grab us some bottled water I picked up while I was out getting her stuff. Her voice carries through my little house as she searches for the cat. "Screamer, come on, girl. Come to Mama."

A few seconds later she comes out of my room with the cat in her arms. I pass her the water bottle and she takes it with a mumbled thank you and plops down on the other end of the couch. The cat lies across her chest and begins purring as she strokes its body with an open palm. *Lucky cat.*

Her eyes averted to the cat, she asks, "You really think that was a bear?"

"Yeah, panthers are quieter and we have a ton of bears out here."

"A gator and a bear all in one day. Well, you don't have to worry about me going down there alone. That scared the crap out of me."

I chuckle. "I couldn't tell until you turned into Flo Jo running full out back to the house."

"I wasn't moving that fast." She rolls her eyes and smiles, still not looking up at me.

"Yeah you were, babe. I was breathing heavy keeping up with you and I'm in damn good shape."

"I've survived too much to end up as bear meat."

"I wouldn't let you end up as bear meat, but it's good that you can run. I really didn't feel like tangling with him today." I tug the knife free from my waistline and set it on the table.

We drink our water and the only sound in the room is that damn cat purring.

"I'm sorry, I—I'm sorry I kissed you. It was wrong," I tell her.

"Sorry?" Her eyes finally find mine and I can see the hurt before she hides it.

"Yeah, that was wrong. You're—"

"Don't," she interrupts me. "You don't need to explain. You're right, we never should have kissed. It was just a weird moment."

Before I can explain that it's not that I regret kissing her specifically, my phone vibrates on the table. It's Mike.

"Hudson," I answer out of habit.

"Summer's been admitted to the hospital. Thomas just called. I'm on my way to the airport to catch the next flight out."

"Shit. What happened?"

"Dehydration and I don't know what else. Fuck, man, I should have gone."

"Don't get crazy yet. Wait until you get down there and see how she is. If you're all wound up when you get there, you'll be a dick. She hates that."

"Fuck, man."

"What did Thomas say exactly?"

"That she was done shooting a scene, it was hot as hell and she collapsed."

"Okay, man. Probably just heat related. I'm sure they admitted her due to her age and pregnancy. Get down there in one piece and find out what's going on. Then you or Thomas call me. I'll go to the office and forward all calls to my phone."

"Thanks, man. I'm sorry."

"Don't be. Take care of your wife."

We disconnect and I scoot forward, preparing to stand and drive into town and do what I told Mike I'd do.

"What's wrong?"

"Mike's wife is an actress. She's pregnant and she's finishing up a movie in Key West. Apparently, she collapsed today and they are transferring and admitting her to a hospital in Miami. I need to run to the office quickly and then I'll be back and we can eat."

Her shoulders slump but she nods and turns her attention back to the cat who is still purring so loud it's surprising that Stacey can hear me talking.

I go back to my room, change my sweaty shirt, slip on some clean socks and tennis shoes and grab my keys. On my way out the door, I remind her, "Don't open the door for anyone. I'll be back shortly."

She glances at me and nods before I disappear out the door. What I can't figure out is how Lawson ever laid a hand on her. Those brown Bambi eyes of hers melt me every time I look into them. They seem to show everything she's thinking, no matter how hard she tries to hide it.

Once I get to the office, I switch the call forwarding to my phone number, grab my laptop, lock up and head back out. I'm only a block from the Lobster Lounge so I swing into their parking lot. I want to have a talk with Mr. Clark, in person, about Stacey's situation.

At the hostess station I ask to speak to the owner privately. She picks up the phone, has a brief conversation with Mr. Clark and leads me through the busy kitchen to a small office off to the side. When I step inside, a tall willowy man with a receding hairline and a long straight nose greets me.

"I'm Hudson McCormick. I'm with Sunset Security. We're new to the area and have an office over on Citrus Avenue."

"Nice to meet you, Mr. McCormick, but we don't need—"

"I'm not here about your security. I'm here for Stacey Allen. She said she filled you in on her situation when she started. She loves this job and wants to keep it, but I had to hide her away. Apparently, her crazy ex has hired a guy who tracked her to town and he was in here sniffing around yesterday. He raided her shithole of an apartment when he couldn't find her. For the time being, she can't come back to work. She was worried about leaving you high and dry for her shifts since you've been so kind to her, but if she comes back, it won't be good."

"How do I know it's not you who has come after her? Maybe I should call the cops."

"If you want to talk to her, you can, her phone is still active; I'm only doing what she asked me to do."

He continues to watch me as he leans back and picks up the phone. A quick glance at a paper on his desk and he's dialing a phone number.

"Stacey, it's Ray Clark. I've got a man here named McCormick."

It's quiet as he listens. "Okay, just stay safe. Come back by when you're ready and I'll find a spot for you."

Another minute of listening and he finally says goodbye and hangs up.

Mr. Clark shakes my hand and thanks me before I head out the door.

When I get back to the house, the first thing I notice when I open the door is the Def Leppard playing in the kitchen and the clink of kitchen utensils. I step far enough inside to get a good view of Stacey's "Pour Some Sugar on Me" performance. Either the music is too loud to hear the door or she's just that into the song. The sound of her voice is slightly goofy but the roll of her body and swivel of her hips is a whole lot of sexy. I could get hard if I stood here too long watching like some creepy voyeur. *Who knew that the 1980's rock anthem could still inspire such a show?* I lean against the wall, enjoying it immensely. Just as she's really belting out the lyrics of the second chorus into a spoon-microphone, she turns and catches sight of me. Her scream scares the cat out of the kitchen back toward my room and the spoon she was holding comes hurling my way, ready to poke my eye out.

"Hey!" I yell as I duck in time for the spoon to bounce off the drywall behind me.

"What the hell, Hudson?" she yells as she stomps over and starts pounding on my chest with her little fists. "Why the hell would you sneak up on me like that, you big jerk?"

I grab her wrists and quickly twist them down and behind her back. Without thinking it through, my mouth crashes to hers. Her little burst of anger turned me on further than her little show did, and I can't help the reaction she brings out in me.

Her body goes rigid against mine, but I ignore it and continue my kiss. Within seconds she's like putty, melting into the kiss, so I release her hands. They come up to wrap around my neck and she opens further for me. *God, this woman is amazing. So sweet, so hot.*

My cock pushes against my zipper and I can't help the groan she draws from me when she presses her sweet, curvy body against mine. I'm certain she feels what she's doing to me. When she pulls away, she whispers, "Hudson," and something about the sound of her voice calling my name against my lips is the perfect catalyst to take this to the next level. I shuffle her over to the couch, sit down and pull her down to straddle my lap on her knees. As soon as our centers connect, I flex into her more. She groans and I shift my mouth to her neck, locating all the tender spots that make her squirm. I forgot how much fun it is to discover these types of things. Usually my sexual encounters are only to get in, get off and get out. But the fun lies in giving pleasure as much as receiving.

My hand slips up under her T-shirt, along her back and she rocks into me. I grip her bra strap to unhook it and pause, waiting for the go-ahead. When she doesn't reply, I pull back enough to see her hooded chocolate eyes and ask, "May I?"

Stacey nods and I groan when I pop it loose. I run both hands up her now bare back and hold her tightly against me. My fingers move of their own accord to the front of her shirt and push the bra out of the way. Her nipples harden instantly against my fingers and her kiss grows more fevered as I work the tight little nipple. The other hand moves to the other nipple and as soon as my fingers pinch that one too, she tears her mouth from mine and throws her head back, moaning loudly.

I'm about to explode in my pants just watching her like this. As I'm about to slip my hand down between us to see how wet she is, the timer on the oven starts beeping. *Talk about horrible timing.*

My hands slide down to her hips and my head drops to the back of the couch. "Son of a bitch!" I groan.

She giggles and scoots away, headed for the kitchen. *Damn buzzer.* A few cleansing breaths later, I reach down to adjust myself. *Shit, I'm going to have the worst case of blue balls there ever was. I need to move before I jump her again.* I stand and step outside just in time to catch the beginning of the sunset. My second favorite thing about this place is the sunsets. I'm out there with my hands in my pockets, breathing deep for only about five minutes when the door opens and she peeks her head out. "Um…dinner is ready."

I follow her inside. "You didn't have to cook for me."

"I know, but I was bored so I thought I'd do it. I'm also pretty hungry."

"Listen, about what just happened."

She stops, but doesn't turn around. Her next statement surprises me. "I know. It was a mistake. I have no idea what keeps coming over me."

I want to beg her not to apologize and drag her back to my room so we can return to the things we were just doing, but I know it's not right. The best thing for me to do is stay away from her. So instead of saying what I want to say, I say what I need to. "Just forget about it and let it go. I promise I'll keep my distance moving forward."

"I'm sorry I hit you," she quietly tells me.

"No big deal. That was like a gnat buzzing around me. It didn't hurt."

"You don't have to be mean about it. But really, I'm sorry. I'm running from a guy who did that regularly. I should know better than to act that way, even if it won't actually hurt you. I was just embarrassed that you caught me in the middle of my Def Leppard concert."

"You in concert a lot?"

She turns and glares at me before making her way to the counter to grab a plate and help herself to a piece of the lasagna she made. "If you would've bought the ingredients, I could have made homemade lasagna. This boxed stuff might clog our arteries in five minutes flat if it doesn't kill our stomachs first."

"I've had it before, it's fine. Besides, I wasn't sure if you could cook and didn't want to assume. What I do know is that I can't cook anything that you are likely to eat. My culinary skills are as exciting as me opening a can, dumping it into a bowl and nuking it."

Stacey flashes me a look of disgust before she shares. "By the time I moved in with Aunt Leona full-time, she wasn't able to do much, so I did most of the cooking and cleaning. I got tired of eating canned everything, so I pulled out her old cookbooks and figured it out. That came in handy when I lived with Lawson because he expected it."

Stacey grows quiet after that statement and I imagine that she's stuck in her head, back in a time that was a whole lot less pleasant. All I know for sure is that if I get ahold of Lawson Allen, I'll make sure he knows how I feel about the way he treated his wife. This woman has obviously had enough shit in her lifetime; she certainly didn't need any more. She needed a man who would protect her and give her the world. Instead, she got a man she needed protecting from and a life of sheer hell. I've got some pretty gnarly things in mind that I could do to him, given the chance.

After she takes her last bite, she asks, "Can we watch a movie or something? I need something to take my mind off all this stuff with Lawson or I won't be able to sleep."

"Yeah, you want to go pick one while I clean this mess up?"

"I can clean it up," she says.

"Nope, not in my house. Rules are if you cook, then you don't clean unless you're the only one around to do both. So, go pick a movie." She nods and heads to my office.

Within a few minutes, the movie is on and she's sitting on the couch in the far corner with her feet pulled up under her. I want to laugh at her. *Does she think I'm going to attack her? It looks like she's protecting herself.* I sit at the other end and rest my heels on the coffee table. Within seconds I'm cursing her for her movie choice. *Sweet Home Alabama.* "Where did you get this shit? I don't own chick flicks," I grumble, pushing my palms into my eyes.

"It was in my bag you brought me. It's my favorite movie and I haven't been able to watch it for ages." When I glance at her, ready to tell her this isn't happening, I notice a sadness that wasn't there earlier. I don't know if she's normally a content person, but for someone who is going through as much as she is, she hasn't really shown sadness. Frustration? Yes. Anger? Absolutely. Fear? Yup. But sadness? Not really.

"Fine. But the next one is my choice." I try to act like a hard-ass, but the truth is I'd probably let her paint my fingernails if it meant she wouldn't look sad again. I'm such a pansy sometimes.

About half an hour into the movie, Screamer jumps up onto the couch and instead of prancing her happy ass over to Stacey, she climbs across my thighs, up my stomach and onto my chest. *What the hell? I'm not a cat person at all.* When I glance over at Stacey to ask her to get this mangy cat off me, her giggle stops me in my tracks.

"If looks could kill, my cat would be dust right now. She likes you. You should show her a little kindness, I don't think she's had much of that."

"You know I'm a dog guy, right?"

"Yeah, I figured as much, but you can be an animal guy for a few minutes and just pet the cat. Look at her…she's staring at you. Maybe she has a slight kitty crush. Don't break her heart."

Groaning, I run my hand from Screamer's head to her rump twice. At the end of the second time, she settles completely on my chest and begins purring. I glance over at Stacey who is smiling at us. *Ah hell, now I have to keep this up.* So I do.

Although I'd never watch this movie of my own accord, it's not too bad. There's some funny shit in there. I've spent a lot of time in Alabama and am able to relate to a lot of it. Carmen's parents are like the parents in this movie and I can't help but smile at that. They're good people whom I've always liked no matter what kind of shit she put me through. It's probably the only reason I've kept an eye on her as long as I have.

At one point, I glance over to find Stacey fidgeting like she can't find the right position. If she wasn't trying to stay stuck to that one spot on the couch, she would do better.

"Stacey, just lay your head on my leg and stretch out."

She's looking at me like I have grown three heads. "I have a cat planted on my chest. It's not like I'm going to try anything on you. You look seriously uncomfortable. Come on, stretch out. I'm not a nice guy often. Take advantage while you can."

She seems to think it over for a moment before she finally readjusts, resting her head on the edge of my thigh like she's trying not to put too much pressure on my leg. After a few minutes, she breaks out into giggles. It's not even a funny moment in the movie. The cat is blocking my view, so I lean a little to get a better look at her. "What is going on?"

"The cat…" She breaks off into more hysterics. "The cat is purring so loud I can't hear the movie. Not a cat guy, my ass." Now she's curled in on herself, holding her stomach as her whole body shakes. I'd love to be irritated by it, but who can be pissed when you get the chance to see her happy like this? She's trouble with a capital T for me. Stacey is ticking off every line on my dream-woman list. A sense of humor and a bit of sarcasm are near the top of that list and she has both.

"Oh, zip it. I can't help it that I'm so loveable." I grin, unable to keep that content, happy feeling from escaping. Such an odd feeling after being unhappy for so long.

She twists her upper body and pushes up on her hand so she can face me. A look of…wonder, maybe, on her face. I hold still as she stares at me like she's trying to figure me out. A tiny smile lifts her lips before she reaches out like she's going to touch my face. Her hand pauses in midair. "You should do that more often. It's breathtaking."

*Never should have told her I'll keep my distance, because there's no way I can, even knowing that being with her in any way puts me at risk of feeling the pain all over again when it fails.*

Her cheeks flush a little with her admission and her eyes lower. Before she can break the moment or I can think too hard, I grab her chin gently but firmly and pull her toward me as I meet her halfway. When I sit forward that little bit, though, the cat spooks and jumps down with a loud meow, like she's pissed. Stacey busts out laughing, and I silence the sound with my mouth on hers. It only takes a half second for her to respond and another two for the kiss to turn into a frenzy.

What is it with this woman? She brings out the beast in me with minimal effort. My body wants to protect her and claim her in a way that's new to me. It's all-consuming and uncontrollable. My mind is telling me once again to stop, but my body is screaming louder, telling me to take her and make her mine.

How did I end up here with a fucking cat who curls up on my chest and a woman, hot and open for me? It's crazy and so unlike me. I haven't done anything impulsive since I married Carmen and reaped the hell that came with that. Every decision I've made since my marriage has been planned to the fullest until I met Stacey.

My fingers push into her curly hair at the nape of her neck and hold her to me. It would take an atomic bomb to separate us at this point. Her arm begins to shake next to my thigh, so I pull back. "What's wrong?"

Her gorgeous chocolate eyes, somehow even darker with lust, stare up at me. "Nothing. I guess it's just the way I'm leaning on it."

I move my hands under her arms and lift her to straddle my lap. *Holy hell, she feels good there.* "Better?"

She nods and runs her fingers along the short hair on the side of my head. "What are we doing?" Her eyes pierce me as her question floats between us. I've only got one honest answer to give her.

"I have no clue."

"Me either, but I don't want to stop." She chews on her bottom lip a little, waiting for my response.

"How far do you want to go?" I ask.

She places both palms on my cheeks and holds me in place, making certain she has my attention. "I don't want to stop. So to answer your question…all the way. How about you?"

## Stacey

Did an alien take over my body in the last few days? Because I'm not acting like myself. This guy gets under my skin. Irritating me, turning me on and making me impulsive and trusting like I haven't been in a long time. Now I'm straddled across his lap with my center pressed against his, waiting for an answer to a question I never thought I'd ask. I pretty much just threw myself at him after spending the last hour and a half avoiding even touching the same couch cushion as him, and now I'm on him, practically demanding sex. *Ugh, how did I get in this crazy situation?*

Hudson studies me carefully. I've never been this bold with a man, never this out of control and certainly never so fearless with the words that come out of my mouth.

He doesn't use words when he finally answers. He leans forward and takes my lips softly, nibbling a little on the bottom one before trailing his tongue across the seam so I'll open for him. As soon as I do, he pulls me in tight to him and stands with me in his arms.

"Legs around me, babe."

I quickly comply and lock him in tight, my mouth going

back to his for more. With a few long strides he has us in his bedroom and my back to the mattress. Before he stretches out on top of me, he strips his shirt off and tosses it to the floor. I swear his big muscles have little muscles of their own. He's perfectly sculpted and smooth until you get to the little trail of hair that runs below his belly button and disappears into his pants. *I bet that happy trail is as soft as it is inviting.* My eyes devour him. Lawson's a big guy, but not as ripped and as well-kept as Hudson. This man is perfect.

"Like the way you're lookin' at me, babe, but I want to make sure you want this."

Hudson's ripped form has left me speechless, so I nod yes.

Ever so slowly he lowers himself to rest between my legs. His body weight held up just enough to feel good, so I won't be flattened under him. A soft moan escapes me when his hips are fully seated between my thighs, pressing against me in the most amazing way. I close my eyes and relish each kiss to my earlobe, neck and mouth. His hand slides up from my waist and over my rib cage, taking my shirt with it. His nose and lips brush across the sensitive tips of my breasts until he snags the edge of my bra cup down with his teeth. Next thing I know, he's nipping at the hardened peak with his lips and rolling it between them. This time I groan, the feeling is so freaking good. He switches breasts, repeating the process while I writhe beneath him. Shameless, I grind against him, hoping to speed things up. I'm wet, needy and so, so, so ready. I don't even remember the last time I had sex when I wanted it, much less this bad.

My hands slip below the waistband of his shorts and boxer briefs to grip the tight flesh of his ass.

"Off!" I beg. "Take them off."

He backs away from me to sit up on his knees and I tug my shirt and bra off, flinging them to the floor. Then, before I can do it myself, he tugs my shorts and panties down. I'm lying in front of him, bare. My skin is flushed and warm, my muscles coiled tight, anticipating what's to come.

He jumps off the bed and drops the rest of his clothes. His cock bounces free and I can't help but think about how good he will feel inside me. Crawling back onto the bed, he lifts my legs onto his shoulders and licks along the seam of my pussy before he opens me with his fingers. He takes a deep breath through his nose and growls like an animal before he gets down to business. As soon as he makes contact with my needy flesh I cry out and flinch. I'm almost too turned on to let him go on.

"Easy, babe. I'll go slower. You just taste so damn good."

I dig my fingers into his hair and grip his scalp, lifting my hips to meet the motion of his tongue. He's in the perfect spot, so it's not too much or too little. The pleasure pressure is growing and my toes curl in response. I'm getting close, so damn close, and he must know it because he stops and crawls the rest of the way up my body. "You ready for me?"

"Yes, please. Tell me you have a condom."

He leans down and runs his tongue over one nipple before he jumps off the bed and digs one out of his wallet and rolls it on. Before I have a chance to complain about how long he's taking, he resumes his position between my legs, hooking one under his arm. I'm wide open and ready for him. He leans down and kisses me, delving deep, tangling his tongue with mine as he pushes inside me hard and fast.

The sudden full feeling pushes me back to the edge he dragged my body to only moments ago.

"More!" I cry out and he begins to move. His thrusts are hard and deep, scooting my body further up the bed with the force of his hips until my head hits the headboard. He pauses to scoot me down and places a hand between my head and the headboard before he resumes the same punishing pace. My hands run all over his back, feeling the muscles flex beneath them until I'm too close to stop the rush. My nails dig into his skin as I cry out.

The sound he releases when he comes reminds me of the bear we ran from in the woods. Loud, feral and primitive. He collapses atop me and he's almost too heavy, but I'm too tired to say anything. I wrap my arms and legs around him and hold tight, hoping that won't be the one and only time I get all that is Hudson.

Once my heart rate settles and reality seeps back in, I allow thoughts of the last couple of days to break through the post-sex haze. If you would've told me a year ago any of this would happen, from Lawson's last beating to hiding in a stranger's house and eventually sleeping with him, I would've laughed myself silly.

The fact that Hudson is a big, strong guy but uses his strength as a protector rather than an intimidator is part of what has drawn me to him. I spent too many years with a big man who used his size to scare me and keep me tied to him. The opposite kind of big man is more than attractive. Not to mention the instant sizzle between us. Maybe it's basic chemistry and pheromones, I don't know. I just know I've never felt anything so powerful as my attraction to him. Sure, I was attracted to Lawson when we got together. He was charming, intelligent and handsome. He hid the lazy, ill-tempered, cheating douchebag side of him until after we were married. But we never had this kind of sizzle and burn between us. I didn't even know this was possible outside of the movies.

That reminds me that outside of this bed is still the threat. A threat that comes from my soon-to-be ex-husband, meaning I'm still married.

He rolls over and away from me to dispose of the condom. When he returns to the bed, he pulls me in close. "What are you thinking about?" Hudson asks as his fingers begin running up and down my arm. My cheek is now resting on his chest, while my arm lies across his rock-hard abs. "Your whole body went from jelly to rigid in just the amount of time it took me to get rid of the condom."

"I'm thinking about how strange it is that I'm lying here with you. I've never been one to sleep around, especially with someone I don't really know. So the fact that I leapt straight into your bed is a little overwhelming."

"Don't overthink it."

"Easy for you to say. You don't look like a big ole slut. I mean, I'm in bed with a guy I just met, and I'm technically still married. Men get away with that kind of thing."

"Only judgmental people think that way, babe, and since I'm the only one who knows, you don't have to worry about that. I'm not judging shit."

His words only make me feel a slight bit better. *He's right, no one knows, and I have no one to tell. Lawson made sure I have no one left in my life.*

"You gonna tell me what finally sent you running? You've been avoiding answering that question."

Exhaling heavily, I pause for a second. I'm sure if he looked into Lawson, he has an idea, but for some reason he wants to hear the words come out of my mouth. He won't know the whole story because it wasn't all released to the public, but after all Hudson is doing for me, I probably owe him an explanation.

"The last week I lived at my house with Lawson, he was in Savannah for his monthly poker game."

"Was he always gone for a whole week?"

"No. His trips down there started extending from a weekend to a week about four months before I left. I suspected there was someone else on the side he was seeing when he was down there, but I never confronted him about it. Number one, I was too afraid to, and number two, if he spent more time away from me, it was more time for my body to heal from his abuse."

"Go on," he urges.

"Well, at eleven o'clock one night, a pipe broke in the kitchen and water was spraying everywhere, flooding the downstairs. Having had no idea where the water shut-off valve was to the house, I called Lawson several times and he kept sending it to voicemail. I got desperate and ran next door to our neighbor's house. Brent was so nice. I'd woken him up and he didn't flinch, he just slipped on his shoes, grabbed a flashlight and followed me to the house. Within 10-minutes he had the water shut off. I said goodnight to him and grabbed the Shop-Vac from the garage to clean up the mess. Without saying a word, Brent came back with his and worked for two hours to help me clean it up so I wouldn't be awake all night doing it myself.

"I'll never forget how kind he was. I hadn't shared more than two sentences a week with him over the couple of years we lived next to him because of my husband, but as soon as I needed something, he didn't even blink." I sigh, hating this part of the story. "Apparently Lawson got my messages and decided to come home and check on the house. When Lawson was surveying the damage the next morning, Brent knocked on the door. Brent thought he was being neighborly by helping and following up, but Lawson accused us of sneaking around and having sex. When Brent tried to leave, Lawson picked up our brass lamp and swung it like a baseball bat. He must have hit him just right because Brent hit the floor and blood went everywhere.

"When Brent hit the floor, Lawson came after me with the lamp to my ribs and his fists everywhere else; eventually I passed out from the pain. When I came to, Brent was still in the same position on the floor with his eyes wide open, unseeing. It was awful. I had no idea how long I was out, so I crawled over to him and tried to do CPR, but Brent was long gone. Noise from upstairs alerted me that Lawson was still in the house. I had no idea where my phone was so I crawled to the door and out onto the sidewalk before I passed out from pain. Thank God my neighbor across the street was coming home from the grocery store and saw me. She came out to help me and called the cops. They were there before Lawson even realized I had crawled out the door."

"Fuck, babe," he grunts.

"Apparently, Brent was dead on contact, so there was nothing I could have done to help him. It's amazing I made it to the sidewalk. I had six broken ribs, a broken arm, a busted blood vessel in my eye, a ton of bruises and I lost my baby."

Hudson's whole body tightens. "Baby? The articles didn't say anything about you being pregnant."

"There were pieces of information that the police kept out of the papers. I have a feeling his family paid some people to keep quiet, just like they greased some palms to allow him out on bail. He should never have been out on bail with the charges against him, but somehow he was. I hauled ass as soon as I could get out of town. Luckily, I'd been planning to leave for a long time and had money and a bag of clothes stashed."

"I'm sorry," he whispered quietly as he held me a little closer. Relaxing a little, I allow the moment of safety to seep into my bones so I can fully relax. He reaches down and hitches my thigh up onto his thigh, pats my butt softly and says, "Get some rest."

I smile and settle in, worn out from the sex and the trip down memory lane.

---

9

Hudson

---

My eyes fly open at the sound of my phone ringing in the living room. I slide out from under Stacey and stride out to answer it. It's Mike.

"Hey, man, how is she?"

"Dehydrated. They're giving her fluids. They want her on bed rest. Thank God she finished shooting her scenes before she went down because there's no way in hell the doctor would allow her to go back to work."

"But she's okay?"

My shoulders relax a little. Summer is a cool chick. Mike's a lucky son of a bitch. I helped him pull bodyguard duty for her last year when she had a crazy stalker after her, and I got to know her a little bit. Since then, I've spent more time around them and Summer and I always get along well.

"Got one problem though," Mike tells me.

"What's that?"

"Summer arranged a surprise for me that's getting delivered today and there's no way to stop it, so I need you to be at my place to receive it and sign off on it."

"Sure, waiting for a FedEx guy is no big deal."

"Not FedEx, dude. Summer went *way* overboard."

In the background I can hear her yelling something about Mike's birthday, which is this weekend.

"So what the hell am I waiting for then?"

"A Robalo 246 Cayman Bay boat."

"Damn. That's perfect for Crystal River and the Gulf."

"She said she knew exactly what to buy by listening to me talk too much about it."

"Anyway, there's no way to cancel the delivery since it's showing up at the house and coming by water. Once she gets there, can you take her out and let me know how she runs?"

"I'm not driving your boat before you do." *He's crazy. That's like riding a man's new Harley before he does.*

"Listen, it would help me out. I need to know if everything is running okay before the guy who delivers it leaves town. If there are problems, he's going to take it back with him."

"This is nuts, you know that, right?"

"Yeah, but I need to be here with her and this was already in motion. He's supposed to be there around 10 o'clock this morning."

"Okay. I'll be there. I'll let you know what's up as soon as I take it out."

"One more thing. My neighbor's kid has been taking Scooter out, but I was hoping you could take him home with you. I feel bad that I left him there alone."

"Yeah, I'll bring the fat hound home with me."

"Thanks, man, I owe you."

"Nah. You know how much I love to be on the river and your dog is easy to take care of."

"When I get back, we'll have to go out trout fishing," Mike says almost wistfully.

"My kind of day."

"Call me later," he says.

"I will." I hang up and slip back into bed next to Stacey.

Brown curly strands of hair tickle my nose as I scoot in close. I can't help but smile at the thought of all her hair. I look forward to seeing what she will look like when she wakes up in a little bit. I think she'll have some crazy attractive post-sex bedhead. I doze back off for a couple of hours until I feel the subtle movement of Stacey as she wakes up. She tries her best not to disturb me; I hate to tell her, but there was no way she would wake up without me knowing.

When I was in the Navy, the guys on my team relied on me to wake up fastest. Someone could breathe funny and I was wide awake. The rest of them could sleep through a bomb on top of our heads, but not me. My mom was the same way.

"You ready to get up?" I ask, my throat scratchy from the couple extra hours of sleep.

"Bathroom," she says.

"You coming back here when you're done?" I ask as she stands up.

"Um…" she hesitates.

"I'd like you to."

She turns fully to face me. "You would?" She's clearly shocked by my confession.

"Yes, I would." I know I shouldn't. More time with someone means more probability of attachment. Which neither of us need. However, that wild hair, coupled with that sweet curve along her waist and ass is too much to resist when I have morning wood and thoughts of the night before running like a film in my mind and usually after one night I'm done. Although, I never bring anyone here. I go to their place or I've even been to a hotel or two, but never here. Everything with this woman since the very beginning has been different. Hell, there is even a cat in this bed with me and I hate cats.

Stacey returns a few minutes later holding a T-shirt in front of her like she's trying to hide. "Are you sure? Just because I'm staying here doesn't mean—" she trails off.

"No, you're right, it doesn't mean anything, so if you want to say no, I'm okay with that, but if it were my choice, you'd drop that T-shirt so I can get a better look at that gorgeous body before you climb back in this bed and let me touch it."

Her lips part and her chest rises rapidly. I can almost see her pulse speed up in her throat. I lift the cover to give her a view of what she's doing to me and the cat skitters off the bed and out of the room. Her eyes lower and take in everything before she smiles shyly and slips back in beside me.

I take her mouth in a deep kiss. A lot of women don't like to kiss in the morning, but the way she's responding tells me that's not an issue for her. I grab her leg and pull it up to my hip and then I shift to my back, taking her with me so her warm, surprisingly damp heat is pressed against me. A little moan escapes between us. She pulls away from the kiss and rises up. Her breasts hang heavily in front of her, her skin flushed with desire. I grab her hand and guide it to her nipple. "Let me watch you."

She circles it with her thumb and I feel myself harden further under her. She must be turned on too because her confidence rises; it's like a switch flips. She places her pointer finger on my lips and orders, "Suck it." *Hell yeah!*

I open my lips and suck her finger between them until she finally pulls it out and uses that finger and her thumb to swirl and pinch her nipple. Her hips buck and she drops her head back. *Holy shit, that's hot.* With her other hand she places the same finger against my lips again and this time I suck and gently bite it before she removes it to tease the other nipple. Her hips grind harder the more she gets turned on, so I slide my hand between us and press on her clit as she rocks and plays with her beautiful breasts. It doesn't take long before her hips are rocking hard and she's splintering apart before my eyes. *Damn, she's sexy.* I reach over and grab a condom from the nightstand and she scoots back so I can roll it on. Once that's done, she rises up and lowers her tight, sweet pussy onto me. *Please let me hold on. I don't want to blow it before we even really get started this morning.* I count in my head before I move, praying the feeling will pass. With her sex appeal and perfect moves, I almost can't control myself. *Am I in high school all over again?*

Her rise and fall is perfectly timed, her hips rolling against mine, and her look of absolute ecstasy is amazing. The overwhelming urge to take control of this has me flipping her to her back and driving deep. Her eyes widen as she bites down on her lower lip. "Yes!" she cries out, so I thrust again. In and out, in and out. Harder each time. Sweat trickles down my back as I fight my orgasm, wanting to keep hearing her make those sweet sounds for as long as possible. I grunt and thrust until I can't take it anymore. She calls out my name as the ripple of orgasm pulses through me.

"Stacey," I shudder and bury my face in her neck. Her legs wrap tight around my waist and I lie there like that for as long as I can. This woman's pussy is like heaven. Her every reaction is perfect. I want to stay in this bed all day long doing this with her, but I know I can't. Finally, I flip to my back and try to get my breathing back to normal.

"That was amazing. I've never been with anyone like you," Stacey reveals.

"Like what?"

Surely she's been fucked hard before.

"With someone who seems to appreciate and encourage every reaction during sex. That helps me relax and enjoy it more."

"I hate to hear that you didn't at least get that from your ex. As beautiful and uninhibited as you are, I don't know how that statement you just made is true."

My head turns to face her and she's blushing, so I wait a couple of minutes before I speak again and change the subject. "Mike's wife surprised him with a boat. Since he's in Miami with her, he needs me to meet the guy delivering it. He asked me to take it out on the water and test it out. Do you want to go?"

Her eyes warm instantly. "Really? You'll let me go?"

"Well, this guy looking for you won't be out on a boat looking for you—that would be a huge waste of time—so yeah, if you want to go. It should be fun. Do you have a swimsuit?"

"Yeah, I brought one of those with me. I haven't been out on a boat in ages. My friend in college grew up on a lake and I went home with her once. While we were there, they taught me how to water ski. It was awesome."

"We will head to their place in about an hour."

"We aren't picking it up at the boat store?"

"No, his wife wanted to surprise him, so she paid to have it delivered by water. Oh, and we're picking up their basset hound to stay with us until they come back."

"Wow, a boat's an awesome present."

"Yeah, Summer's pretty awesome all the way around."

Something strange flashed in her eyes for a second, but before I could ask what it was, it was gone. "They have a basset hound? I figured him for more of a Labrador or German Shepherd guy."

"Scooter is a rescue dog. Mike wasn't looking for a dog when he got him. It just sort of happened."

"I love dogs. I wanted a couple, but Lawson wouldn't even consider it."

*If she were mine, I'd give her 10 dogs if she wanted them. That guy has no idea what he had when he had it.*

10

Stacey

We got showers, fed the cat and then headed out the door. I had no idea what to expect going to Mike and Summer's house. I was surprised to find that they were renting a little place on the river. I thought with her being a movie star they would have some mansion with three stories of crazy luxury or something, but it's a modest, older two-bedroom home that's been remodeled. When we reach the front door, a horrible howling sound, like an injured dog, can be heard coming from inside. "Oh my gosh, Hudson, you have to hurry up. Their dog is hurt!" I feel a little panicky at the thought of a dog in pain. I have the softest spot for animals.

"I know it sounds bad but he's probably okay. If Mike is gone for too long and no one is around to pay attention to him, he makes that sound. It's how Mike found him."

"I can't stand it. He sounds miserable."

"It'll be okay." He turns the lock and opens the door. The sound stops instantly and Scooter, the chubbiest basset hound I've ever seen, comes running out to greet us.

"Hey, buddy!" Hudson bends down to scratch the hound

behind his ears until Scooter notices me and slips away from him. Hudson's powerful thighs flex as he stands and I almost have to wipe the drool from my mouth. Scooter nudges my shin, so I bend down to scratch him. "You were right. He's fine. Must have been really lonely."

I stand and move all the way inside and then bend over to pet Scooter again. "Wow, this place is nice."

Hudson replies, "They're looking to buy a three-bedroom, two-bath soon, but didn't find exactly what they wanted to buy when they were ready to make the move, so they decided to rent for a bit. It is a nice house." He pauses a second and continues, "I think you'll be surprised when you meet Summer in person. She's not your typical Hollywood starlet. She's so down-to-earth."

I nod, thinking about what he's saying. I guess if you don't make it big until you're older, you understand the necessity of being humble.

When we step out back with Scooter leading the way, his belly practically dragging along the grass, to wait for the delivery guy, I see why they rented this house. It's on a little canal around the corner from Kings Bay, right off of Crystal River. Although you can see boats going by down at the mouth of the canal, it's a serene little spot. The backyard is mostly shaded by a huge old oak tree that's growing in the middle of the small grassy area leading up to the seawall. Just beyond that is a wooden dock that runs alongside a covered boatlift. The houses on the other side of the canal are all different colors, shapes, sizes and ages, adding to the unique variety in the area.

Just as the sweat evidence of a humid Florida summer slides down my spine, a beautiful, new, center console boat turns into the canal and heads for the dock. The side reads Robalo in silver lettering on the almost all-white boat. The center console has a windshield and a roof equipped with four fishing pole holders. The whole thing is white against the water, except the bottom third of the boat, which is royal blue. Seats make up the area in front of the console, making it the perfect boat for a day of fishing, swimming or even scalloping. A small man with a huge brown and gray mustache, wraparound sunglasses and an SFG baseball cap is driving the boat. When he pulls up to the dock, Hudson helps him tie off the boat and Scooter and I stand back and watch as they both work efficiently. Once the boat is situated, Hudson introduces himself and shakes the man's hand. I give a small wave from my place on the dock.

The man points out a few things on the boat to Hudson and they talk for a few minutes while I continue to admire the boat, excited to get out on the water. He hands a card to Hudson and says, "Call me if you have any issues. I'll be in town for the rest of the afternoon. Y'all have fun!" The man grins at us as he struts down the dock and through the side yard to the front where he disappears.

"Don't we need to take him back where he came from?"

"Nah, someone was picking him up out front. Come on, let's take her out." I scoop the heavy dog up and Hudson helps us onto the boat. I move to the front and sit Scooter down on one of the cushions next to me. Hudson unties everything and turns the motor on. Then he moves us away from the dock and begins the slow pace toward Kings Bay. Because of the large manatee population in this portion of the river, the speed limit is lowered to 2-3 mph. We tour Kings Bay and then head down the river. I strip off my shirt to get some sun and sit back to take it all in. *This is heaven.*

"You mind if we head out to the Gulf? I need to run this thing wide open," he yells to me.

"Sounds great to me," I reply with a smile. I glance over at Scooter, whose ears are blown back a little as the breeze pushes at them. He barks once like he agrees and I stroke his back. Hudson follows the boat in front of us and when we pass the sign marking the end of the no-wake zone, he throttles the engine and the wind whips around us, helping to alleviate the perspiration that built up during the required slow zones on the river. Once we're out quite a ways, Hudson slows the boat to a stop and drops the anchor. Off to our left you can see some boats that dot the horizon line, and to the right the smoke stacks from the power plant have white columns of exhaust rising toward the heavens.

"Want to jump in and cool off a little?" he asks as he strips off his shirt. I'm stricken dumb for a second as I take in the bulging muscles of his shoulders and pectorals. I wonder if I would ever get tired of seeing him without a shirt on. The sight is so amazing I can't imagine that I would.

"Hello." He waves his hand in front of my eyes and I know I blush bright red for being caught eyeballing him.

He steps in close and lowers his head so his mouth is close to mine. In a deep husky voice, he asks, "You like what you see?"

My heart flutters madly behind my ribs and I lick my lips, unable to stop the inevitable. I nod a little and rise on my toes to press my mouth to his. This kiss is slow and deep, simmering my organs in my overheated body. A loud bark startles me and I pull away abruptly. Hudson and I both turn to find the dog watching us intently.

"I don't think Scooter likes you paying attention to someone else." He smacks me on the butt playfully and says, "Come on, let's cool off."

Next thing I know he's doing a cannonball off the bow of the boat. Water splashes back onto Scooter and me and it feels amazing. I shimmy my shorts off my hips and place them on the seat and follow him in.

The water is perfect and when I come up to get some air, I

find Hudson smiling at me, that same exuberant smile he had once before, and I wonder if he used to flash that smile easy and often before life pulled him down. It is natural on him and it warms me despite the coolness of the water.

Before I can think to say something, he dips under the water and shoots toward me like a torpedo. I squeal and try to get away but he is too fast, grabbing me by the waist and pulling me under. We both surface again and I splash him playfully, giggling until he starts tickling me. Then the squeals begin again as I fight against him, which triggers Scooter to start barking. Hudson finally stops and flips over to his back to float. For such a big guy he can float with the best of them. I study him as I tread water, the sun glinting off the ridges and planes of his muscles. Every part of him is a work of art, beautiful and powerful. But the most amazing part of that scenery for me is the look of sweet contentment he has on his face. Eyes closed, facial muscles relaxed peacefully, and his lips have a slight upturn toward them, like he's simply enjoying the moment for what it is. *I doubt he has many of these moments.* Instead of ruining it with words or actions, I simply flip to my back and take up the same position. I can see why he has such a peaceful expression because that's exactly what this is. The water mutes the sound of other boats, the sun warms my skin and the weightless feel of the water is heavenly. I feel his hand reach out to hold mine and we float there like that for what feels like both a minute and forever.

Finally, we sit up and swim a little before returning to the boat.

Once we are back on the boat the mood between us is mellow and he seems more approachable. "So, since you know a lot about me and I know almost nothing about you, do you mind if I ask some questions?"

"Knock yourself out," he says as he stretches out across

from me on the cushions of the bow, soaking up the sun beating down on us.

"How did you get that scar on your forehead?"

"I'd love to say it was something tough like I got it in a bomb blast in Afghanistan, but I can't. Our family was camping at Ginnie Springs State Park when I was 12 and my brother, Cally, was 10. We decided to go exploring on our own and found a rope swing by the river. Neither of us ever had any fear, so we decided to try it out. Apparently the rope was dry-rotted, and since I went first, it snapped before I got far enough out to be safe to drop in the water. I smacked my head on a jagged rock and busted it open. I also broke my arm. Blood was everywhere. It was bad. Anyway, I had over sixty stitches."

"You have a brother named Cally?" That's an odd name.

He must suspect what I thought of that because he adds, "His name is Callahan. We were both named after towns in Florida. My mom's kind of a nut like that."

"What's your family like?" I've always been fascinated by families since I only had one for a short time.

"They're good people. Mom and Dad own a hardware store near Cedar Key and travel when they have time off. Both are native Floridians and are very proud of that fact. They also fish and hunt together in their time off."

"Your mom does too?"

"Oh, yeah. She's into all that stuff. Probably enjoys being on the water more than anyone I know. She can sit for hours with a fishing pole."

"I've never been fishing before."

He turns his head to look at me. "Really?"

"Really. No one around to take me. Aunt Leona was too old and fragile." I shrug and turn my face back to the sun. My childhood wasn't horrible, wasn't great either, but it's times like this I realize the things I missed out on.

"I'll have to take you," he says. I smile to myself, thinking I like that idea.

"So, what does Cally do?"

"Air Force. He's a pilot."

"Your parents must be proud, both of their boys serving their country."

"My dad was in the Army during Desert Storm and was not thrilled about his boys joining up, but yeah, they're proud. We were hell-raisers, so it's good that we went into the service rather than prison. I wasn't college material and Cally wouldn't have been either, but he knew he had to graduate to be an officer so he could be a pilot in the military."

"Do you have any other family around?"

"Yeah, tons of cousins, aunts and uncles. Both sets of grandparents are gone though." There was something sad in the way he said that.

"Were you close to them, your grandparents, I mean?"

"Yeah. Spent a ton of time with both sides, but my dad's dad was the best man I've ever known. He died while I was in Afghanistan the last time."

Somehow I know at that point that question time is over so I quiet down and just enjoy the feel of the sun and the sound of water sloshing lightly against the hull of the boat.

The rest of the afternoon is spent riding around the Gulf and finally back up the Crystal River, talking about the houses and the people who live in them. If ever there was a perfect day, today was it for me. I couldn't have felt better or been more relaxed on a spa day.

The sun is midway in the sky when we pull back up to the Wade house. I lift Scooter onto the dock and he trots over to the grass to do his business while we tie the boat off and shut everything down. Within minutes we're inside Mike and Summer's home, gathering Scooter's bowls and food when

Hudson's phone rings. His eyebrows draw low as he hits the answer button.

"Gene," Hudson says as he answers the phone and listens intently for a moment. *That's weird, I wonder who Gene is.*

"Myrtle, oh Lord," Hudson's voice is low, almost hoarse, his face suddenly twisted in pain. He backs up and sits in a chair by the dining room table and lowers his head so I can't see his face. He's quiet as he listens to whatever is being said on the other end of the line. His shoulders tense up and his whole body grows rigid before my eyes. *What's going on?* Out of instinct, I place my hand on his back, hoping to show support and give some level of comfort. It's dumb to think a hand can soothe whatever has him like this, but it feels wrong to stand there and stare at him without doing something.

"Okay, I'll see what I can do. It sounds like she's beyond any help we can give her, but I'll do it for you and Gene. Take care of yourself, Myrtle, and I'll check in. If something changes, please call me."

He clears his throat as he hangs up and lowers his hands between his legs as he keeps his head down.

I wait a minute before I quietly speak. "Hudson?"

He takes a deep breath like he's steadying himself and stands up, shrugging away from my touch. I can't help the wave of hurt that ripples through me at his rejection. After such an amazing day of feeling comfortable and confident with him, our little bubble of beauty has obviously burst. Striding over to the counter, he grabs his keys. "Can you get Scooter's stuff. I need to take you two back to my place. I have something to take care of."

"Are you okay?" I ask, confused as to what happened. *What changed in a two-minute conversation to bring the coldness back into him?*

"No, but I will be. Come on, I need to get going." Gone is the warmth and fun we shared all day long. That's been replaced by the stranger I encountered outside the trailer that first night. *What in the hell was that call about, and who are Gene and Myrtle?* Just like everything else in my life, the good moments are few and far between and the goodness for today is over.

The ride back to his house is silent except for the panting of Scooter, who is sitting in my lap looking out the window like he wishes it was down. When we finally pull in front of Hudson's house, I'm practically choking on the discomfort of the situation.

I set Scooter in the grass and grab his leash, leading him around the yard a little so he can sniff and mark his territory a few times. Once I feel his time outside is sufficient, I lead him inside through the front door that Hudson has left cracked for me. When I get inside, I unclip the leash and let him roam.

There's a tense moment when Screamer spots him, hisses and finally runs away to hide when he barks at her. Hudson's nowhere to be seen. In a house as small as this one, disappearing is a difficult thing to do. Just when I'm about to yell his name, he returns from the garage carrying a shotgun case and several boxes. He pulls the shotgun out and inspects it, sets it back in the case, closes it and sets it off to the side. Then he disappears into his room and comes back out only a moment or two later in a pair of black cargo pants and a new, plain black T-shirt, carrying a pair of boots with him. Dropping the boots next to him, he grabs his hunting knife and clips it to his waistband, pulls a handgun out of a case, shoves the clip in the bottom of it and puts it in the waistband at the back of his pants. He shoves ammunition and a few other weapons I'm not familiar with in a black backpack and throws it over his shoulder. He returns to his room and switches out his blue and gray SFG hat for a black one, slips on combat boots and walks toward the door. He looks like he's going to war. He pauses at the door and looks back at me.

"Lock up behind me. Only go outside to let the dog out

and come right back inside. I don't know when I'll be back, but you have enough food for a few days."

*A few days? He's crazy! I can't be stuck here alone waiting for him, not knowing what's going on for more than a few hours. A few days is completely out of the question.*

"What's going on?" I ask, panicking as I rush toward him, ready to hold him in place if necessary. *What if he gets hurt? What if he dies? I have no idea how to get back to civilization and nowhere to go.*

"The less you know, the better." His eyes have lost the warmth of last night and today and I hate the chill his tone sends down my spine.

"Are you kidding me?" My panic attack is coming on at a high rate of speed and I lose it. "You drag me out here to the middle of nowhere. Have sex with me…repeatedly. Take me out on the water and act like we're dating all day long. Then you get a cryptic phone call, shut down on me, treat me like a stranger all over again, and now you're loaded up in more gear than Rambo and leaving me here alone? You must be crazy!"

Hudson closes his eyes and swallows like he's trying to push his irritation down. Meanwhile, my whole body is shaking with anger as my mind races with negative possibilities.

"The less you know, the better. I didn't mean to treat you like shit, but that phone call reminded me why I don't get involved with women anymore, and as you can tell, I was way too involved these last 24-hours."

He may as well have just slapped me with an open palm after the words that came out of his mouth. My eyes narrow on him. "Then why bother bringing me back here? I can take care of myself, have been for a while now."

He chuckles humorlessly. "If you could take care of your-self as well as you're saying, I would never have gotten involved in the first place or had to bring you out here. When I get back, we will get your shit straight and you can go back to South Carolina."

Without waiting to hear my response, he exits out the front door and I hear his truck fire up and pull away. A scream of frustration and anger rips through me and echoes around the small living space. Scooter trots out from one of the rooms and barks at me. *How did I end up in this situation? Why do men always feel like they can treat me like shit? I'm so tired of allowing myself to be treated this way. Because in the end it is my fault; I allow it.*

*You know what? Screw him. He doesn't control me. I won't leave because who knows how long Scooter will be stuck in the house alone, but I'll be damned if I sit back and let him dictate my every move even when he's not here, just like Lawson did to me.*

I go back to the office, grab my tennis shoes and slip them on without socks, grab Scooter's leash and clip it on him. Then I walk out the door and head for the creek with Scooter sniffing every bush and sprig of grass along the way.

After about 20 yards I finally slow my pace, realizing that Scooter's basset hound body can't seem to keep up with my angry strides. When we get near the pond, I watch carefully for gators and see none today. Thank God, because I bet a dog Scooter's size would make a tasty snack for one of those guys.

When we finally reach the creek, the dog walks right up to the water and dips his head to drink. His long ears drag in the creek, making me laugh. I sit on the same big rock I did last time, strip off my shoes and soak my feet in the cool water. It doesn't take long for the serenity of the place to calm the turmoil in my head.

The more I think about things in a calm state, the more I realize that Hudson didn't really do anything wrong by me except be a dick before he left. He doesn't owe me anything. I'm just a woman he found who was in need of help. He helped and I opened my legs. I can't say it wasn't good for me because that would be a huge lie. It was fantastic. He never promised me anything, he never acted like anything more was going on with us besides what was, so I had no right to feel angry by his words.

Do I forgive him for being a dick? He hasn't asked to be forgiven so I suppose it doesn't even matter. When he finally comes back, I'll just ask him to take me to my car and I'll locate a shitty little motel to spend a day or two in until I decide where I'm moving to next. It's no big deal, or that's what I keep telling myself.

After spending far too much time sitting there contemplating my mental state and what I will do next, I begin putting my shoes on. A crack of branches upstream a little draws my attention. Two of the cutest little black bear cubs roll out toward the creek, almost like little boys wrestling, the way they're tumbling around together. As cute as they are, I know by their size that their mama can't be far away. I tug on Scooter's collar and start briskly moving back the way we came, hoping he doesn't start barking at our visitors. When I think we're far enough out of sight, I slow down so he can catch his breath and then we continue back to the house at a much slower pace.

Once we're back inside, I get Scooter and me some water and I sit on the couch contemplating what to do. It's not long before I decide I need a comfort read, something I've already read and know I love. I can't concentrate on a new story today with all the turmoil in my head; but that's okay because Kaylee Ryan does a good job of taking me to my happy place when I read *Beyond the Bases*. I grab the worn-out paperback copy of the book and stretch out on the bed.

Just as I'm getting comfortable, Scooter barks, so I lean over the side of the bed to find him staring at me with those soulful eyes, his tail wagging almost as if he's waiting for me to pick him up. I don't know if Hudson will care that a dog is in his bed, but it doesn't bother me. He was a jerk to me, so I don't care what he thinks. I pull the fat hound up on the bed and roll to my side to read and he curls up right into my belly. Within minutes I'm immersed in the book as he snores against me. Two chapters into the book I feel the bed dip slightly and when I turn, I find Screamer staring at Scooter in extreme distaste. It doesn't take her long to grow tired of giving the stink-eye to the dog and she climbs up to the top of my pillow and curls herself around my head. *This is new, but I'm guessing if I could pick her little brain, I'd find it's her way of being proprietary of me.* I go back to reading my book, lost in the world that a beautiful mind created for me.

# 11

# Hudson

I've been all over town looking for Carmen and her skank-ass pimp. I can't believe this is what her life has become. It's sad and ridiculous and absolutely heartbreaking. Myrtle called to tell me that Gene's in the ICU. They don't know if he'll make it. They couldn't get Carmen in a treatment facility for a week, so they were doing their best to detox her and keep her under their roof. She said it wasn't going too badly until her pimp showed up, shot Gene and dragged Carmen out of their house by her hair with the help of some huge redneck enforcer. Apparently, she'd called him, wanting him to get her some more smack, promised him she'd go back to whoring for him if he came and got her.

After the pimp shot her dad, though, she wasn't as willing to go with him, but he'd already lost a ton of money on her previously, so he was there to get payback. Myrtle said it was horrible. She was calling to ask me to track down the man who shot Gene. She said she'd given up on Carmen, but she wanted justice for her husband. I never could tell those people no and I understand where Myrtle is coming from. They're good-hearted, hard-working, God-fearing people who deserved better than the lot they'd been given in life.

That phone call snapped me back to reality and made me wonder what the hell I was doing screwing Stacey and taking her out on the boat like a couple dating. That's just stupid. I don't want a relationship. I don't want the responsibility of having to save another woman. I just want to get up in the morning, handle client needs, hang with Mike, travel a little, when I'm not working and just...be. I don't want to be concerned about anyone else and I don't want the heartbreak that follows when it all comes crashing down, because it always does.

Now I'm sitting in my truck in front of my dark office at two o'clock in the morning, contemplating if I should go inside and work on this or get some sleep and come back to it fresh in a few hours. While I was asking questions at the beginning of my search, I was told the guy I'm looking for is Sly Jenkins and if he doesn't want to be found, he won't be. I agreed to disagree on that front. I guarantee he's never had a former Navy SEAL on the hunt for his ass. I did get a line on a property that he usually takes his girls to, but hours of surveillance on that place turned up nothing. Moving forward to find Sly, I need to quit working on emotion and sit down to craft a strategy. This is a small town, one where people still know almost everything about everyone and I should be able to use that to my advantage somehow.

When I originally set out to find him earlier, I was hopped up on more than one emotion. Anger at Carmen for putting her parents in such a dangerous position, one that may have gotten her father killed, and disappointment in myself for treating Stacey like shit. I know it's wrong, but the truth is that Carmen taught me that I don't ever want to get tangled up with feelings again. It wouldn't take much with someone like

Stacey. Her twisted combination of neediness and strength is mind-bending and perfect for me, but I can never trust my gut when it comes to the opposite sex again. Apparently, all logic falls out of my head and disappears when women are involved.

Finally, too tired to focus, I give in to going home and grabbing a few hours of sleep on the couch to clear my head before I head out again.

When I pull up to the house, I can see the lights are on in the kitchen, living room and my bedroom. *That's weird.* I tiptoe down the hall to my room. When I step inside, I'm halted in my tracks. Stacey's in my bed, fully clothed, lying on her side. Scooter's curled into her stomach watching me, but not moving. The cat is wrapped around Stacey's head, her paws buried in Stacey's hair, asleep. *She must have been reading and fell asleep because the book is still mostly open and lying half on her face.* I almost laugh at the sight. It's adorable in a way I don't like to notice. I wish nothing about that warmed my gut. I flick the light off and step closer to Scooter. "Do you need to go potty, big guy?" He lifts his head, so I pick him up gently, hoping not to disturb her, and set him on the ground. He follows me to the living room where I locate his leash and clip it on him.

After taking him out to do his business, he gets a drink and trots back to my bed where Stacey is still sleeping. I lift him up and he curls back into place. I lift the book from her face and move it to the nightstand. The cat wakes up and lifts her head to stare at me but doesn't move any further. I grab a small fleece blanket from my couch, drape it over her and go back out to shut off the lights and lie down on the couch.

*Why do I have to be so damned attracted to her? I'm never going to be able to sleep with the image of her resting in my bed. Why does it matter what her skin smells like, what her legs feel like wrapped around me or how she responds to every touch and kiss I provide her? It shouldn't matter. No. It doesn't matter. It can't. If I stay away from her until I get her issue and Carmen's issue taken care of, I'll be good to go. Shouldn't be hard if I leave her here and work from the office.*

THE NEXT MORNING I'm up and out of the house before Stacey and the animals even stir slightly. I only got three hours of sleep to be able to make that happen, but at least I didn't have to see her sleepy doe eyes and bed-mussed hair this morning. That would have fucked with my head all day. As I'm turning down Citrus Avenue, I get a call from my buddy outside of Charleston.

"Hey, man, you got a minute?"

"Yeah, you caught me on my way into the office," I tell him as I turn off the truck and jump out.

"The guy you called me about is Billy-Jack Mullens. He may look cheesy, but he's a bad-ass motherfucker. He's been doing this work most of his life, and word on the street is that most of the time he doesn't capture to return, he captures to kill. They say he's a fan of torture, especially when it comes to women. Lawson Allen hired him six weeks ago when she disappeared. I'm still not sure how he tracked her to that location because I haven't found any trace of her that he may be following, but somehow he did. You need to keep her locked up until you can get ahold of him. But make sure when you go after him, you plan for all scenarios, because if he gets you at a weak moment, you won't have another chance. He'll kill you and not look back. He's wanted in three states for murder, kidnapping and a slew of other heinous shit, and law enforcement can't seem to get their hands on him."

"Did you find Lawson in your hunt for Mullens?"

"Nope. He's in the wind, but if I were a guessing man, I'd say he's not far from Mullens. He wants revenge and he wants to dole it out himself."

"Shit. Thanks for the information, man."

"You got it. If you need backup, let me know. I can be down there in five or six hours."

"Thanks." I disconnect and sigh as I make my way through the office, flipping on lights. I sit down at my desk and do a search on Sly Jenkins and find his given name is Sylvester Tyrone Jenkins. He has a chunk of property out in Homosassa and a home in Crystal River. *I've already staked out the Crystal River home. It's time for some recon in Homosassa.*

I've got the local map spread out on the desk in the small conference room we have at the end of the hall and my laptop set up with the satellite view of the property Sly owns when I hear the door open. I lean my head out the conference room door to find Thomas coming down the hallway.

"What are you doing here?" I ask.

"Mike isn't leaving Summer's side, so I thought I'd come back and see if I could drum up any business here."

"How's Summer?"

"Her blood pressure is elevated so they are keeping her for observation. I imagine they will send her home in the next day or two, but it sounded like she's on bed rest for a bit. So, what are you working on? May I help?"

I lead him into the conference room and explain the two major things I'm dealing with now, and I watch as Thomas' eyes light up. He's a danger junkie. He gets off on the adrenaline spike with situations like this.

"Do you want me on recon for Sly or tracking Mullens? Or we can work both together?"

I think about it for a minute. It's probably better to take each guy on together since neither are amateurs.

"Let's do them both together. We'll start with Sly and then work on Mullens. He won't be leaving town without her and I know she's safe where she is now, so we can take care of Carmen and then Stacey."

"Stacey at your place?"

"Your brother tell you that?"

"Yes, and it's the only place you could hide someone where no one would look for them."

"Yeah, she's at my place with her damn cat and Scooter for now. I need her out of my place sooner rather than later, though, so I want to wrap this all up as quickly as possible."

He stares at me like he's assessing my last statement and I do my best not to squirm. We're guys, we don't talk about our feelings, so I doubt he will say anything if he understands what's going on, but I don't want to chance it.

"Let's get our shit together so we can get out on Sly's property."

⸺

IN LESS THAN TWO HOURS, we're hiking across to Sly's property through several large, privately owned parcels of land. My truck is waiting for us at the house of a farmer Thomas paid to pretend he never saw us.

The Florida heat coupled with the humidity is a killer in full fatigues and combat boots but it's necessary to stay camouflaged as we move in close. It also protects against all the damn insects out here. With the radio earpieces in place, we are able to communicate as we separate. He moves to the south side of the property, which is the front door and driveway, while I monitor the back door and porch.

"I've got eyes on the front. A black Land Rover and a black Lexus are parked out front. No activity."

"Roger that. Eyes on the back. No activity."

We stay quiet and I stretch out on my belly in the brush and settle in to wait. I learned a long time ago that patience is important in these scenarios.

A LITTLE OVER three hours later, a tall, skinny African-American man in a baggy T-shirt and jeans and a short, stocky, Hispanic man with a huge gold chain around his neck, wearing baggy jeans and a wife-beater step out back. Before the door to the house shuts, the Hispanic guy tugs on a chain that looks like a leash and a seriously emaciated Carmen stumbles out the door behind him. I can see him yelling at her as she cowers at his feet, but she doesn't seem to respond. She's in a different shirt than the last few times I helped her, but she looks worse than before, if that's even possible.

Both men light up cigarettes and flick the ashes at Carmen. She doesn't even flinch. She's so far gone she doesn't even care anymore. They must have shot her full of something. *I wonder if she even realizes that she may have gotten her dad killed. The better question is, does she even care?*

"I've got eyes on one black male over six foot tall and slender. I believe it's Sly. There is a Hispanic guy with him. Probably five foot seven, one hundred and fifty pounds. He's got Carmen hooked to a dog leash at his feet. They're smoking cigarettes and talking."

"Roger that. A red Mustang just pulled up and two teenage boys got out. Wannabe thugs. They're banging on the front door. Door opened, but I can't see who answered. Those two are going inside."

So that tells me we have more people inside. How many, though, is the question. I stay comfortable where I'm at and wait. We need more information before we go in there.

Once darkness falls, Thomas creeps up to the house, gets a look inside and reports back that there are six people, plus Carmen inside, and by the sounds of it, one of them is the big redneck enforcer. Every time they come outside, Sly comes out with the same guy and Carmen on the leash. The last time, she was more out of it than before, so I'm sure she's been given more, but at least that part is consistent.

"Next smoke break, we take out Sly and his minion and extract Carmen."

"Copy that," Thomas says in my ear.

# 12

## Stacey

*That bastard. He really left me here, stuck in this house last night and all day long. I'm losing my mind. At least he left me some food this time, but I can't believe he hasn't even checked on me. I want to walk out the front door, down the dirt road and find civilization, but if I do that, then I'll be leaving Scooter and Screamer behind. I can't do that to them. It's not their fault I ended up in this mess.*

It's dusk and I'm restless so I put the leash on Scooter and step out into the muggy Florida air. It's cooler when the sun is setting, but not enough to keep me from sweating. I'm not quite ready to run from the bear cubs again, so I set off down the dirt road that leads off the property. The dog makes sure to sniff every inch of grass along the fence on the side and lift his leg every two or three sniffs. Once we get to the main dirt road, we make a right and follow it until we finally tire and sit to rest. Well, more like Scooter gets tired and refuses to walk anymore, so he plops down and I follow. It's dark on this road and although I enjoy looking up at the vast number of stars I can see, I'm also thankful for the moon that illuminates the lonely area we're seated in.

The headlights of a vehicle approach and I look around,

trying to figure out where I can hide. I didn't realize anyone was out this far besides us. *Shit. I have nowhere to go. I couldn't get Scooter over or under that fence and I won't leave him here.* Choosing to remain where I am, I hope maybe the driver won't notice me.

My luck is obviously not that great because the car pulls up to me and the window rolls down. My stomach clenches tight, my nerves now in overdrive. A woman around my age rolls the window down. "Do you need help? Are you okay?"

Scooter barks once. "Oh, I didn't realize you had a dog with you." She flashes him a friendly smile and his tail wags.

"Yeah, we're okay. He doesn't want to walk anymore, so I'm just letting him rest."

"Do you live around here?"

"No, I'm staying with an old friend." I wasn't sure what else to say, so hopefully she buys that.

"Well, I can run you home. The critters could be out running around after dark. I'd hate for one of them to come after your cute little dog."

I look down at Scooter who is standing, ready for his ride like he understood everything she said. *That probably isn't a bad idea.* "Actually, that would be really nice. We aren't far, but he's not going to make it. I forget he has little legs and a big belly, not a great combo for long walks."

She giggles. "Come on, jump in."

When I open the door and the overhead light comes on, I see that she has the most beautiful head of auburn hair I've ever seen. As soon as I'm seated with Scooter in my lap, she says, "I'm Shay, by the way. I live on the property behind this one but we're having our driveway paved, so I have to cut through the back way right now."

"Hi, I'm Stacey. Thanks for the ride. If you turn at the next driveway, that's us."

"Oh. You're friends with Hudson? He's such a great guy!"

"You know Hudson?"

"Yes, he and his partner helped me out not long ago and my fiancé is about to start working with them. He got hired right before Mike left town. Do you know if they've heard anything about Summer?"

"Mike's wife?"

"Yes. Isn't it crazy that we have a movie star living right here in town?"

"This is their dog. We're dog-sitting until they get back. I think she's okay, but I don't know any more than that."

She comes to a stop in front of Hudson's dark house. "Well, it was nice meeting you—"

"Stacey. It was nice meeting you, too. Thank you for the ride."

She reaches over and scratches Scooter's head before I climb out of the car. She stays there with her car lights on the house until I get inside and turn on a light. *What a nice person. A lot of people around town seem to be like her. It's part of the reason I wanted to stay here in the first place.* Screamer darts into the living room and begins sharing her ire about being left behind without food. I go into the kitchen and scoop her food into her bowl and do the same for Scooter. They eat side by side, not even glancing up at each other with their muzzles buried in their bowls.

It's while I'm getting them both fresh bowls of water that I hear the telltale sound of Hudson's truck pull up. I don't stop to greet him when he finally comes through the door. In fact, I go to the bathroom to avoid contact with him. As I'm washing my hands, I hear his voice talking to someone and curiosity gets the best of me. I dry my hands and step out into the living room.

Hudson is leaned over someone, trying to adjust their limp body.

"Damn it, Carmen. You've got to help me. If you puke on this couch, I'll put your ass outside."

Carmen's answer is a mumble. I move closer and realize I'm looking at the same woman from the night I met Hudson. The woman on the couch is in worse shape than when I first saw her, and she smells. I can't tell if it's feces, vomit or both. Either way, it's gross.

"Can you get me the trash can with a fresh bag, please, Stacey?" he asks without saying hello or looking up at me.

"Yeah," I grumble, and I return a minute later with what he requested. He sets it next to her and stands straight up.

"Can you also get me a wet washcloth?"

I do that too and hand it over.

Finally, he turns his focus to me. "I need you to keep an eye on her. I'm still not sure what I'm going to do with her yet, but I couldn't trust her to stay in the truck."

"What do you want me to do with her?"

"Make sure she doesn't die. Keep her on her side in case she vomits again and don't give her anything but water. We should be back soon."

"I don't know how to take care of a junkie!" My voice raises with every word. *He's leaving me here alone again in the middle of nowhere with a drug addict who doesn't look like she will live through the night, with the directive, 'Make sure she doesn't die'? Is he crazy? I didn't survive one hell to be shoved in another headfirst.*

"I don't have time to explain, but I have to get to Thomas who was tracking a guy through the woods in Homosassa." He turns and runs out the door, and I'm left looking at Carmen, the druggie, as she lies drooling on the couch passed out. *How did my situation go from bad to worse in a matter of days?*

A few days ago, I was on the run from an abusive, psychotic husband, and now I'm staying with some guy who is dealing with a druggie and expecting me to keep her alive. I'm an idiot when it comes to men.

I'M AWAKENED in the early hours of the morning when I hear the front door open. I've slept lightly, waking to every sound, afraid Carmen would either stop breathing or slip out while I was asleep. Although she never looked like she was ready to trudge out into the night and walk a bunch of miles to civilization, I wouldn't put it past her drug-addicted tendencies to try.

I climb out of bed and lower Scooter to the floor. The cat stays on top of my pillow and only bothers to crack one eye open in the process. Stepping into the living room, I find Hudson leaning over the back of the couch observing Carmen. He straightens and finds me standing there with my arms crossed over my chest, both angry and tired.

"I want you to take me back to my place," I tell him quietly.

"No." He brushes past me into his room and begins stripping out of his clothing. It's then that I notice he's not just covered in mud and debris, he also has a bunch of little cuts and scratches and probably some areas that will be bruises tomorrow.

"You don't have a choice. You can't keep me here against my will," I tell him, defiance thick in my voice.

"Please let me shower and then we can discuss it. I'm running on about three hours of sleep, I'm dehydrated, and I'm out of patience. You can wait five minutes."

He doesn't wait for me to respond as he turns and enters the bathroom and starts the water.

He infuriates me by dismissing me so easily. *I've been here alone, because I certainly don't count the druggie, and when I tell him I need to leave, he blows me off for a shower.* I plop down on the bed and breathe deep, trying to control my emotions. I know I'm being unreasonable. This guy has given me a safe place to stay for free, but because we mixed sex with this scenario, I'm confused and hurt. I'm not the kind of woman who can have casual sex, so I don't know why I did. I can chalk it up to emotions running high or being in a crazy situation with a man who looks like Hudson. But in the end, the only truth is that I'm an idiot.

A couple of minutes later, Hudson comes out of the bathroom, followed by a room full of steam, wearing nothing but a towel around his hips. *Now I remember how I ended up in this situation.* His sexiness factor on a one-to-ten scale is a fifteen. It's ridiculous how stupid I become in his presence.

He steps over close to me and guides me to my feet.

"I get that you're pissed. I didn't plan to be gone that long or leave you with Carmen, but I needed her safe and I needed to go back and get Thomas. We got our guy and turned him in to the sheriff's department."

"I still want to go back to my place. I can figure my stuff out tomorrow and take off on my own."

"That's not going to happen." He steps in closer, his voice quieter, and I squirm a little.

"Why? That's what I want." My eyes narrow and I do my best to act pissed off, despite the heat flaring between us.

"Because it's not safe. The guy with the Camaro is Billy-Jack Mullens. He was hired by your ex to track you down. Apparently, he's well known for his torture and kill tactics. Until I find him, you can't go back to your place. I don't want anything to happen to you." I'm getting emotional whiplash dealing with Hudson's mood swings. I don't know what is going on in his head.

He tucks my hair behind my ears and smooths the rest down and away from face. He slides his fingers under my chin and gently lifts it. My lips part and I can see the desire in his eyes. "I told you I'd take care of you and keep you safe. I'm not done yet. Yesterday I was distracted." He presses his lips to mine and I melt into the kiss.

I rationalize my stupid behavior by saying to myself I'm

just lonely after being left alone for so long, after months of loneliness on the run, and years of loneliness in my marriage, but in reality, I like him way more than I should.

It's almost as if I'm on the Bipolar Express, between his mood swings and my headspace when it comes to him. Running out the front door and never looking back would be the best choice, but as usual, my body is betraying me and choosing the worst path.

When he kisses me again, I open for him and deepen the kiss. Goosebumps raise along my arms and legs. The strength in his arms is soothing as he wraps them around me, pulling me closer to him. Breaking away, I kiss along his stubbled jaw, down his neck to the valley between his bulging pectorals. My nails scratch lightly across his nipples and he growls.

With a few quick movements, he has my back to the bed while Screamer is scrambling to get out of the way, screaming as she goes. We both chuckle and go back at it again, but this time his mouth is on mine as his hands tear at my clothes to get them out of the way. You would think snatching his towel off would be easy, but he's working so hard to get my clothes off that I can't reach his towel. Once I finally yank it free, his damp torso, slightly sticky from the hot shower, presses against mine and I moan in anticipation. I know what's coming and I want it so bad. He reaches out and snags a condom from the nightstand and rolls it on. Then he pushes inside me to the hilt and I arch against him, absorbing the burning stretch and enjoying the fullness. He adjusts my ankles to his shoulders and pushes up on his powerful arms so he can watch as he pumps in and out of me. After only a few minutes I cry out, shaking and convulsing with pleasure and he rolls to his back, taking me with him.

After that, I'm ready to curl up and slip off to sleep, but he doesn't seem to be close. Gripping my hips in his hands, he guides me to a rhythm he likes. He pierces me with his hooded stare and never looks away. I roll my hips while his hand comes up to cup my breast, fingering the sensitive nipple. My hand slides to the other breast to mirror what he's doing. His eyes flare when he glances down to see what I'm doing, and I feel him swell more within me. Knowing that he likes what he sees urges me on and I keep going as I increase my pace. My thighs are burning, my core is ready to boil over and my heart is ready to explode. Hudson's lips purse and he grips my hips harder than before and begins to hammer up into me, almost throwing me off him. "You've gotta come, Stacey!"

I'm close so I dip my finger between us and circle my tightly wound bundle of nerves that are waiting for attention. Within seconds I'm exploding and he's following me. I fall forward and bury my face in his neck as we both work to catch our breath. Once our heart rates have settled a little, Hudson taps my butt to move. He ties off the condom and tosses it to the trash can before adjusting so he's halfway on and off me. He kisses my shoulder softly and whispers, "We will talk in a couple of hours. I'm beat, babe."

Tired and pliant from great sex, I answer, "Okay," and drift off to sleep.

A few hours later I awaken to cussing coming from the living room. I reach over and find that Hudson is out of bed. The cat is back on my head, but Scooter must have slept in the living room because we never lifted him to the bed after sex last night. I'm a little achy all over, but in a good way. As I'm sitting up, Hudson comes through the door looking like he could skin someone alive.

"What's wrong?"

"She's gone."

"Who?" *He can't be talking about Carmen. She couldn't even lift her head last night.*

"Carmen," he growls as he tugs his running shoes on and stalks out of the room.

I spring to my feet and tug on a T-shirt that was lying on the ground as I follow him.

"How?"

"Walked, I guess. Can you take Scooter out? I need to go look for her."

"She couldn't have gotten far, judging by her physical state last night."

"Who knows with her. I should have dumped her ass off at the police station with Sly, but I wanted her to see what she did to her dad before I turned her in. She needs to see what she's doing to the people who love her."

He pulls the front door open. "How long will you be gone?"

"Until I find her, I guess," he says as he shuts the door behind himself.

Scooter whines at me and I go put on clothes and flip-flops to take him out. We spend 20 minutes outside, allowing him to do all his business. Afterwards, I take him inside and feed both animals before I get cleaned up for the day. I'm hoping Hudson will come back and get me so I'm not stuck here inside all day again. I'll go bonkers.

# 13

# Hudson

Carmen is either going to send me to the brink of insanity or be the death of me. I'm not looking forward to either, but it's inevitable with the shit she pulls. I got her out of that house where they were keeping her doped up and caged in a dog crate, making her eat and do her business as if she were a dog. *Even a junkie doesn't want to live that way, so why would she leave my house still all fucked-up just to likely end up right back in that?* All the years of dealing with her bullshit has me hating her. *She had no idea I was taking her to see her dad so that can't be why she ran. As far as she knows I only turned in Sly. Maybe she thought the police would come after her. Whatever it is, she's caused a kink in my plan for today and I'm pissed.*

I was wrung out last night when I came home and found Stacey in my house pissed off and ready to leave. I would have said and done anything for her to stay at that point, even though I told her earlier that we aren't together and I don't get involved with women. I allowed myself to give in to all the things I was feeling, and I should regret it, but I don't.

One thing seeing Carmen like that yesterday did for me is give me a kick in the ass. I needed that reality check. Stacey may have a truckload of issues, but she's not Carmen. She's a fighter, someone who wants to live and love. The only reason she left her husband is because he treated her like a punching bag. She could have turned to drugs to cope but she didn't. She found a way out and is fighting for a future.

Now I just have to figure out how to undo what I've done with Stacey. I need to spend a little time explaining my revelation and what my initial issue was. Probably more than anything, I need to apologize, which is not my strong suit. However, I need to find Carmen and get her to the authorities. I should have known better than to leave her on the couch unattended, but I thought she was finally bad enough that she wasn't going anywhere for a few hours at least. I've always underestimated her, never seeing how far into Hell she could drag the people who love her. Last night was no different.

I've been all the way down the dirt road in all directions, also down to Highway 19, and she's nowhere to be found. I know she didn't venture into the brush or the woods because she's terrified of bugs and wildlife. Even in her questionable state I know those fears are so ingrained that she wouldn't chance an encounter. *She must have called someone again.* I didn't notice a phone on her, but it could have been in her pocket. She's always been resourceful, so I wouldn't put it past her to have one on her or grab one of ours.

Finally, I give up and call Thomas as I drive back to my house. "Hey, Carmen is gone."

"What do you mean 'gone'?" Thomas asks like he can't believe it.

"I left her passed out on the couch last night after I picked you up, and she found a way to wake up and take off."

"All the way in the boondocks? No offense, but that woman has a serious death wish."

"My guess is she went back to Sly's people since they can provide the smack. She was in bad shape, probably can't go very long between hits anymore," I tell him more irritated than anything at this point.

"That's what I'm thinking."

"I have to jump in the shower and grab Stacey. Then I'll be at the office for a bit. Can you meet me there? I need to find Carmen. This time I'll drive straight to the local sheriff's office and drop her sorry ass off there. This is the last time I'm dealing with her. Originally, I wanted her to see what she'd done to her parents, but I don't think she would get it, or care, and I know it will hurt her mom."

"Yeah, I'll grab a cup of coffee and meet you there."

We hang up as I pull in front of the house. Stacey opens the door but stops to stare at me as Scooter pushes past her on his leash, ready to go out. *I guess I have some fixing to do to make this right.*

Stacey looks down and walks to the opposite side of the front yard. I walk up close behind her, slipping an arm around her waist and kiss her shoulder. She turns her head quickly, tickling my nose with her hair.

"I'm sorry," I tell her with as much sincerity as I can convey.

She doesn't move except to look at me over her shoulder.

"I was a complete dick. Now you see what my choice in women has gotten me for too many years. Carmen is the only serious relationship I've had since I was in high school and she's caused nothing but pain in one form or another."

She switches the leash to her other hand and turns all the way around to face me, concern etched in every feature.

"You've heard what my choice in men has been like. We aren't that different. We both made shitty choices and paid for them. When I left my house in South Carolina, I wasn't looking at ever getting involved with anyone again. I have no idea what happened when our paths crossed, but I can tell you it hurts when you're a jerk. I don't deserve it, and—"

"Shhh," I put my finger to her lips. "I know and I'm sorry. I want to try this again. Please be patient with me. I have to find Carmen and deliver her to the local authorities, but after that, I'm free and clear of her. Give me a chance to prove to you that I deserve a chance."

Her eyes soften before they smile, and I love the way the brown turns from dark and angry to light and sweet. I've never seen anything like it before.

"On one condition. You can't leave me here. I don't care if I'm tromping through the swamp with you to find her. I can't stay here alone again today. Please."

I know it's wrong. She shouldn't leave this property until Billy-Jack Mullens and her husband have been found, but after everything over the last couple of days, I can't say no to her. In truth, I don't want to leave her behind either. "We still have to keep you out of sight. We can't go sit down and eat. We have to stop at my office, but otherwise we'll pull through the drive-through at some point."

"I can deal with that. I just can't stay cooped up anymore. I walked the dirt road with Scooter the other day and met your neighbor, but Scooter didn't make it far."

"Neighbor?"

"Shay. She said you did some work for her not long ago. I think you mentioned her when we went to the creek too."

"Yeah, she and Paxton, her fiancé, are good people. In fact, Paxton works for us now. Do what you need to do to get ready for the day and then we can head out."

"Okay, it shouldn't take me long if I can wear shorts, a T-shirt and a ponytail."

"You can wear whatever you want as long as you keep that gorgeous body covered. I don't want Thomas to get any ideas."

She starts to laugh and I kiss her hard enough to stifle the noise and draw a moan instead. Then I smack her ass playfully. "Don't get me wound up, woman. I need to take care of this."

"Eeeep!" she squeaks and hurries into the house, giggling the whole way and leaving me to wonder why I would ever try to push someone like her away.

In less than an hour, we're bouncing down the dirt road back toward my office in Crystal River.

When we arrive, Thomas is already there, seated behind Mike's desk with a coffee cup sitting next to the computer keyboard.

"Hey, man."

"Hey." He glances up and catches sight of Stacey and his face splits into a huge flirty smile. *He better lose that before he addresses her or it's going to be a long day.*

"You must be Stacey." He stands and offers his hand to shake.

Her return smile is brilliant, and a pang of jealousy hits me right in the gut. *Damn, I'm not usually jealous, especially of a guy like Thomas who I know wouldn't slide in under the radar with someone I'm seeing.*

*Wait.*

*Did I just say 'seeing'? Where did that come from? I've slept with her a few times and might be interested in more, but nothing is set in stone yet. I need to slow this down a bit.*

When their handshake lasts a little too long for my liking, I glare at Thomas until he releases her hand, a wicked grin upon his face. *That bastard knows what he's doing to me.*

Before I can say anything to him, my phone rings.

"Hudson."

"Hey, it's Josiah Brown."

I excuse myself and take the call, half distracted by their murmured conversation in the next room. By the time the conversation is over, I realize that Thomas and I are going to have to leave town for two days in the middle of all I have going on. I want to decline this time, but we are just starting this business and I need to be responsible about this, especially since Mike can't leave Summer right now. *Fuck. There couldn't be worse timing.*

When I re-enter Mike's office, Thomas and Stacey are chatting away happily.

"What's up?" Thomas asks.

"That was Josiah Brown. He needs us to fly to Miami this afternoon and be there for two days. He has an emergency meeting in Europe tomorrow and his wife has a charity gala she has to be at."

"Both of you have to go?" Stacey asks.

"Yes, he wants two men on her when she's in public and wants us to rotate sleeping shifts. It's only two days. I can't turn this down because this business is so new, and he stands to be a regular client if things go well. Are you going to be okay for two days at my place?"

Because I know she hates being cooped up out there, I'm afraid she'll try to take off on her own, and I don't want her to get hurt, but most of all I don't want her to leave.

"Yeah, sure," she says, but I can hear the waver in her voice. She's going to go bonkers at my house with no contact for two days.

"Mike and Summer will be back here and can go out and check on you," Thomas says. "The doctor is allowing her to come home and be under the supervision of her doctor here."

"Um, yeah. That's great. That's good, okay." She's rambling, so I know she's trying not to make me feel bad about it, but it's obvious it still bothers her.

"Okay, I'll talk to Mike and find out when they'll be back and when he'll be over to check on you. I'll also give you his number in case there's a problem," Thomas says, doing his best to be helpful.

I focus on Thomas. "I'm going to get her some things from the store and pack. I'll meet you back here to drive to the

Tampa airport at three o'clock. When will Paxton be back in town?"

"He might be back tonight. I'll check the schedule and let you know."

"He and Shay can check on her if he's back. Their property butts up to mine so it won't be hard for them to do."

"Okay, I'll see you this afternoon. Do you want me to have someone else find Carmen while we're gone?"

"Nope. She's going to have to wait."

He nods like he understands. I could call a friend from Security Six in Tampa to track her for me while we're gone, but it's probably good that I don't get my hands on her now. I'm still so damn pissed at her for leaving when I went to all that trouble to save her ass again. I'll worry about her when I return. What I'll do in the meantime is check in and see how her dad is doing. No news seems like good news, but I hate to assume.

———

AN HOUR later we're back at my house and I'm packing while Stacey lies on her side on the bed with her head in her hand, watching.

"You actually wear a suit?" she asks as I zip up my black tailored suit in a hanging bag.

"Yes, when we have high-profile clients, we have to attend functions that require a suit or a tux."

"It has to be tailored to fit with your shoulders and neck. I don't think you can walk into a department store and buy one off the rack."

I laugh out loud. "No, definitely not. I hate wearing them, but if I was wearing a poorly fitting one, that would be its own form of torture."

"So, who is this supermodel you're going to babysit?"

I can't be certain but I think there might be a bit of jealousy lingering in her eyes.

"It's my client's wife. Celebrities seem to get a special kind of dedicated weirdo, so I don't blame him for taking extra precautions. Mike's wife had a crazy stalker. That's how they finally got together. They were friends for years until that whole thing went down. Let's take a walk to the creek before I have to leave. You'll want the fresh air and I'll feel better about leaving if we do."

"Okay, sounds good."

We put a leash on Scooter, but instead of going out through the front door, I pull the blinds back from the sliding glass door and point to the middle of the doors. "Flip that piece of plastic down and pull the broom handle out of the track and this door will open right up. I should have shown you this the other day, but I forgot about it because I never use this entrance. Also, the window in my room is low enough to the ground that you could climb out if you needed to."

Her eyes widen. "Why are you telling me this stuff?"

"So you're prepared if you need to get out of this house some way other than the front door."

"Now I'm a little freaked."

"Don't be freaked. It's just smart to be prepared. Come on, let's get this walk going."

Twenty minutes later we're at the creek. She's stripping off her socks and shoes while Scooter's ears drag in the water as he drinks.

"I love it here. If there weren't so many critters running around out here, I'd come here every day."

"When I get back, I can teach you how to handle yourself so it's safe for you to come down here. I'll also talk to Shay about taking you to the part of the creek that runs through their property. If you think this is pretty, you won't want to leave that spot."

With my shoes finally off, I wade in after her and pull her in close to me. Scooter's leash rubs against my calves as he trots through the water behind me.

She wraps her arms around my waist and smiles up at me. "You aren't the asshole I first thought you were."

"I'm not usually an asshole. I'm blunt and I'm quiet and I hate when people, especially women, put themselves in harm's way, so I have a hard time hiding my irritation when that's happening."

"That's a sexist remark."

"Listen, I was raised in a very Southern family. Women are respected and revered and we protect them even when they prove they don't deserve it. My granddaddy always said his job in life was to protect and love his wife and family. There wasn't a day that my granny or anyone in my family didn't feel we had those things from him. I also never met a more well-mannered, respectful man toward women, although my dad is a close second. Those are the kind of role models I have. I do my best to follow in their footsteps; it's been hard with Carmen, but in general I try to be that guy."

"That was a lot of words from a guy who claims to be quiet." She smiles at me like she's teasing.

"I speak when I have something that needs to be said. Otherwise, I just stay to myself."

"Got it. So you didn't like me because you thought I was putting myself in harm's way?"

"The first time I saw you I was fighting crackheads to get Carmen out of another shitty situation. The second time I saw you I was surprised to see you at the Lobster Lounge. The third time I saw you I was pissed that such a beautiful woman was putting herself in the position to get hurt. So yeah, I guess it was hormones and irritation from then on. It's as if you have no idea how sexy you are and that makes you a bigger target for all the idiots and freaks running around in this world."

"You think I'm sexy?" She grins at me and her eyes shift to my mouth. The things that grin does to me...I almost can't control myself.

Instead of answering with words, I close the distance between us and consume her with a kiss, pulling her flush against me so she can feel how sexy I think she is. *Damn, I'm an idiot. I should be pushing her away and running for the hills. The way she makes me feel is potent, the thought of her is all-consuming and the taste of her is completely addictive.*

The kiss grows deeper and more frantic and I'm certain that if we weren't in the middle of the creek in the woods, we'd be on the ground devouring one another. I finally pull back to get a handle on things. Her lips follow mine, obviously not ready to let go, so I place a few chaste kisses across her cheek to her ear. "I can't take you right now, especially with the dog here."

"Damn," she whispers and giggles.

"I need to head back so I can get to the airport on time."

She nods as I release my hold so we can get our shoes back on.

---

NOT TOO MUCH LATER, we're back at the house and I'm pulling away as she stands out front, waving as Scooter barks. As much as I want my business to succeed, I'd rather stay here and finish what we started in the creek.

## 14

## Stacey

When he was pulling away, it didn't feel like a two-day good-bye. It felt like forever. I hope that's just fear and not some kind of sixth sense. When I was living in my crappy little place on Eighth Avenue, I would go several days at a time without seeing a soul. A couple of days alone with a cat and a dog should be a breeze. I think the problem, though, is not that I'm alone, it's that Hudson's not here. *How did I go from being pissed at him constantly to practically falling in love with the guy? Something is seriously wrong with my head.*

Scooter and I take a short walk up the driveway to the dirt road and back. Then I take up residence on the couch and spend the rest of the afternoon and evening reading.

———

I SPEND the next day cleaning. His place isn't filthy, but it's not exactly clean and I need to be up and moving for a bit. After that, Scooter and I take a walk to the dirt road and back, and finally I return to my book. Hudson has called once to check on me, keeping the call brief.

"Babe, you doing okay?"

"Yes. Bored, though."

"I'll make it up to you when I get back tomorrow night. Mike was delayed and won't be by to check on you until later this evening. Summer is having a rough ride home. He said they've stopped for her to puke a few times already."

"Tell him not to worry about it. I'm okay. He needs to take care of her. It's quiet out here."

"See you tomorrow night," he says quietly.

"Yeah, see you tomorrow," I return. Then we disconnect and I go back to reading.

———

A FEW HOURS LATER, I'm sitting on the couch reading. Screamer is lying across the back of the couch snoozing and Scooter is resting in front of me on the floor. Suddenly, Scooter raises his head and growls. So far, I haven't heard him growl, didn't even think it was possible. "What is it, boy?"

I swing my legs off the couch, my feet now touching the floor, grab my sneakers and slip them on in case I need to take Scooter out again. He climbs up from his place on the floor, trots to the front door and paces, growling the whole time. Something is obviously going on, so I creep over to the front window and peek outside. I don't see anything and just as I'm about to go back to the couch to wait it out a little longer, I hear it. The sound of a dual exhaust muffler. It's down the road a little, but close enough to be heard and probably about ready to turn down the driveway. I return to the window and look outside, and that's when I see the black Camaro with its lights off turning down the driveway.

*That's bad news. It's the guy who was waiting for me outside my house when Hudson brought me here in the first place. How did he find me?* I try to call Hudson, but it goes to voicemail, so I hang up and shove my phone in my back pocket.

Scooter begins to bark as the sound grows closer. I run to the bedroom and snag a bedsheet from the linen closet, my phone and Scooter's leash. "Come on, boy! We've got to take a little trip." I hustle to the back door and unlock it like Hudson showed me. Then I snatch Scooter off the ground and slip out the back door as quietly as possible. Screamer will hide under the bed and be okay in the house, but Scooter could get hurt. The car shuts off out front and I take off running toward the creek. Billy-Jack doesn't even know I'm here, so it shouldn't be any big deal. I can just wait him out back in the woods and pray that no animals get us in the meantime.

Just as I'm nearing the pond, the back door flies open and it's loud enough that I hear it, so I turn back, and to my horror I find him sprinting toward us. I run as fast as I can while holding the fat little dog in my arms. My heart is pumping wildly, fueled by fear and adrenaline. Once I cross the tree line I pause, set Scooter down, whip the sheet out and fashion a sling that ties over one shoulder. Then I shove Scooter's body down in there, only leaving his head out. "Now you be quiet, boy; we have to hide. If this guy gets us, we're probably dead." His long tongue reaches out and swipes my cheek. I don't hear anything, but I glance back anyway out of fear. He hasn't breached the tree line, so I turn and hustle through the woods toward the creek. As soon as I hear the trickling of the water, I slow and carefully work my way around the roots that line the ground until I'm around the backside of the biggest tree. Then I squat down and rest against the trunk, hoping he was too scared to come back in here.

I have no idea how much time has passed. I'm sweating with Scooter's hot little body pressed against mine as we wait. Voices cut through the silence and I hold Scooter's snout with my hand to make sure he doesn't bark. *More than one person is out here? Holy shit! I thought it was only that Billy-Jack Mullens guy.* My phone is buzzing like crazy in my pocket but I'm afraid if I grab it, I will make noise and alert them to my presence. The beam of a flashlight cuts through the darkness in front of me toward the creek and I stay as still as possible. Lawson's voice can now be heard. *Oh my God! He's here too?* My legs begin to shake at the fear of these two sadistic horrible men finding me.

"There is no way she's back in this shit, man. I know her and she's too scared of her own shadow to attempt being back here," Lawson yells.

"Fuck off, man. I saw her disappear into these woods. She's here; she's just good at hiding. Now keep looking. This job has already lasted longer than I wanted to invest," Billy-Jack complains.

"You're getting paid, so quit your bitching," Lawson snaps at him.

"Seems like you owe me more now."

I can tell by their beams of light and splashing feet that they cross the creek, and I hold my breath, praying neither of them look back and see us. My heart is hammering in my chest so loud it seems like they should be able to hear it even though they're further away now. They venture down the little path where the bears came from the other day and I breathe a sigh of relief. I'm so glad they're getting away from here. I can go back to the house and call for help on my way. I stand and work my way around the giant oak and manage to keep quiet until the last step when I trip and land on my hands and knees in the mud, trying to avoid squishing Scooter.

A beam of light comes from the path toward the house and I panic, trying to get away.

"Stacey!" a male voice calls to me and suddenly there are hands helping me up. When I stand, I'm looking up at the outline of Mike, Hudson's partner, and some guy I've never seen before. Scooter must smell Mike because he claws at the wrap like he's trying to climb out, sniffing loudly and whining.

"You've got Scooter in there?"

"Yeah, I couldn't leave him there for those guys to hurt. They're assholes; they might have killed him."

"You really are nice," he says and smiles at me as he reaches in to pet Scooter.

"Who is following you?" the other guy asks.

"Billy-Jack Mullens and my ex-husband. They went that way," I tell them as I point the direction they ran off in.

"Pax, hang tight and I'll take her back to where she can see the house. Then you and I will go in after those two guys."

My body locks up as fear sets in. "There's a family of bears back in there."

"I'm sure there is more than that," he replies as he's ushering me back toward the house.

"No, I mean, I've seen them. A mama and two babies. I don't know about any others. Hudson says there's a limestone cave they live in back there."

"Okay, we will keep our eyes peeled. When you get to the house, call 9-1-1 and lock everything up until we get back." We hurry through the brush until we get to a point where I can see the house.

"Be careful, please," I plead with him, worried something will happen and it will be my fault.

"We've got this. Now go!" he urges, and then he turns and runs at a full sprint back into the tree line, disappearing into the dark.

By the time I get back to the house, get Scooter unwrapped and give him some water, my nerves are shot. They're practically vibrating with fear. I turn off all the lights and sit in the dark with the curtain pulled back in Hudson's room, watching the dark field by the lake, hoping to see movement. It feels like I'm waiting forever when I finally see something. The problem, though, is it's so dark that I can't tell who or what it is. I squint harder, hoping to make sense of the shape coming in the direction of the house. Right then a banging on the front door startles me and I jump back from the window.

"Stay here, Scooter," I tell him as I shut him in the room and rush to the front door. He lets out three loud, quick barks and goes silent. "Quiet, Scooter, I don't want them to know you're here."

"Open the door, Hudson! They're after me!" a female voice screams, and the pounding continues. *Oh my God, that's Hudson's ex! Someone's chasing her all the way out here? I can't leave her out there.* I run to the front door and realize there's no peephole. The screaming continues, sending fear spiraling through all my muscles.

I can't leave her out there to get hurt, it doesn't matter how much of a mess she is, so I swing the door open, expecting to let her into the safety of Hudson's house. Instead I'm greeted with Carmen hunched over in front of a short, sinister Hispanic man. "Get inside, you dumb whore," he grunts at her, and it takes a beat too long for me to figure out what's going on and try to shut the door on them. Realizing what I plan to do, he sticks his foot in the doorway and shoulders his way in, pushing her to the ground ahead of him like she's nothing more than a piece of garbage. She's so drugged out and beat up that she doesn't immediately get off the floor and out of the way, and I trip over her, trying to get past.

"Where's that asshole who turned my partner into the cops?" he spits at me as he moves his attention from Carmen to me.

"I–I—have no idea what you're talking about," I stumble over the words.

"That big motherfucker. You know, that asshole you're shacked up with?"

"I don't know. He left town on business yesterday." I raise my hands higher, hoping he'll stop waving his gun so erratically.

*Where are Mike and Paxton? God, I hope that was them coming back through the clearing. I don't think I can deal with Lawson, Billy-Jack and this guy all at once. I'm barely holding on as it is.*

"Get on your knees, bitch," he grunts at me and I comply. "Hands on top of your head. Don't move an inch."

I do as he says, but my hands are shaking so bad I'm afraid he'll take that as moving.

As he's pulling something out of his pocket and muttering to himself, voices can be heard outside the front door. *God, please let that be Mike and Paxton.*

"Stay there!" the Hispanic man barks at me. "Don't move or say a word!"

He throws the front door open and steps into the doorway, ready to fire on anyone standing there.

Mike and Paxton stand there with a severely injured Lawson draped over their shoulders, carrying him between them. They're all covered in blood and look like something out of a horror movie.

"What the fuck?" The Hispanic guy keeps his gun pointed at the men. "You know what? I don't care. Just get in here!" he yells at the three of them. My gut churns, because even though Lawson is hurt, the old fear I had of him is enough to cripple me completely. He lifts his head and opens his eyes, staring straight at me, and the hatred is so heavy, I shudder. However, I don't dare move because I know the Hispanic guy is still trigger-happy and really angry.

Mike speaks first. "Who're you?"

"Don't matter. What matters is you do what I say. I want

that motherfucker who turned my partner into the police. He's going to pay for costing me so damn much."

Paxton glances around the room, seeming to catalog every little thing, ending with Carmen practically passed out on the floor next to me. My arms are aching from holding them up on my head so long.

The Hispanic dude points his gun at Lawson. "You the motherfucker who turned Sly in to the cops?"

I can see why he would think that. Lawson is thick, a big guy like Hudson.

Lawson spits blood onto the floor and glares. "The only person I plan to kill is my wife."

Mike lets his support of Lawson go and he lists to the side until Paxton lets the other side go too. When Lawson hits the floor with a thud and a grunt, I can see more injuries. It looks like razors scraped down his back from his shoulders to his butt more than once. Lawson groans as he tries to prop himself up to see me. He may be injured, but he's so determined to hurt me that I can't help the shaking that's taken hold of my body.

"Told you I'd find you," he growls before Mike puts his combat boot into Lawson's back, forcing a scream.

"Shut the fuck up!" the Hispanic guy yells to everyone. "If he's not the one, where is the asshole I'm looking for?"

"In Miami. He left yesterday afternoon," I squeak, hoping it will make him leave.

He steps closer to me, focusing all his attention on me. "When will he be back?"

I don't answer, too afraid to speak, so he swings and hits me in the side of the head with the gun. "Ouch!" I cry out and my hands fly to my head where he hit me. By the level of pain I'm feeling, I almost expect to find a big dent in my head where he hit me.

"It'll be worse than that if you don't give me some real answers!" he yells, clearly losing his tolerance. He hits me again and this time I fall half on Carmen and she groans. The Hispanic guy bends down to get in my face, but he didn't realize he left his back to the two guys standing when he lost his temper. That was a grave mistake. Mike leaps across the room and brings an elbow down hard on his head and he crumples to the ground, but not before he squeezes the trigger and gets a shot off with the gun. I scream so loud that Scooter starts howling from the bedroom, making the worst sound I've ever heard, and it takes me a minute to settle down and realize it wasn't me who was shot. It's Carmen. Right in the side of the neck. I scramble to get to her as blood sprays all over the place. I strip off my shirt and push it against the wound, hoping to stop the bleeding. It's gushing out at an alarming rate and her wide, frightened eyes are pleading with me, practically begging me to save her. Pax holds Lawson down while Mike gets the Hispanic guy under control.

"Call 9-1-1! Oh my God! Call 9-1-1!" I shout in a full panic.

"We called when we were coming back. They should be here soon. Just hold that as tight as you can to her neck and talk to her."

"Carmen, don't die on me. Hang on. You've been through so much, you can make it through this." I plead with this woman I don't even know because I don't think I could stand it if someone dies right in front of me. Especially with my hands on her. I know she's a drug addict, but it seems like such a waste. I keep babbling nonsense stuff to her and finally the first of two ambulances comes rumbling down the dirt driveway with their sirens blaring.

A paramedic rushes through the door and over to kneel next to me. He takes over the pressure on her neck while the other moves in on her other side. A third one tries to get answers from Paxton about what happened. A second set of paramedics moves toward where Lawson is lying on the floor.

More sirens can be heard as they pull in next. Several police officers come inside and while they're trying to get the story from us about what happened, the paramedics load Carmen on the stretcher, rush her out to the ambulance and pull away. The second set of paramedics works on Lawson, and the whole time he's cussing and screaming at me. "You'll pay, you stupid bitch!" is the last thing I hear from him as they place the oxygen mask on his face.

Mike tells the policeman closest to us, "That guy is wanted in South Carolina for murder and assault. Also, he hired a man to track his soon-to-be ex-wife and has threatened to kill her several times in front of us."

"Did y'all do that to him?" the officer asks as he points to Lawson's mangled legs and back.

"No, we actually saved him from the bears. The other guy wasn't as lucky. You'll find him when you go looking. He was the one hired to track her down and abduct her."

Shock sets in and my world moves on in slow motion, with the lights flashing outside the window and open door. It's as if I stepped outside of my body. Almost like none of it really happened, like I'm in a dream. It takes a minute before I finally sit down on the ground right in the middle of the room. My legs just don't want to hold me and my mind can't take another minute. *What the hell just happened? A drug dealer, my ex-husband, bears, a drug addict, a gun and so much blood. Did that seriously all just happen?* It's too much. I pull my legs up close and wrap my arms around them, trying to hide or something.

Mike rushes over, putting a hand under my chin and lifting it gently so he can look into my eyes. "You okay? Did anyone hurt you?"

*Yes, someone hurt me*, I want to scream. But somehow, I know he's talking about my physical state and not about my emotional state. Getting hit hurt, but I'm okay. I shake my head, not really able to respond verbally yet. It just all feels like too much.

"No one hurt you? Or no, you're not okay?" he asks to clarify.

"I'm okay," I whisper, unable to say more. Lawson's muffled scream of pain rings out as they lift the gurney and take him outside to the ambulance.

"Come on. Let's get you up on the couch. They can question us where it's more comfortable. When they're done, we can grab Scooter and go to my house. I'm not leaving you here tonight." He leads me inside with a comforting arm around my waist.

"Screamer," I say.

"What?" he pauses in front of the couch looking confused.

"My cat, Screamer. I can't leave her here. She's in the bedroom with Scooter."

"Okay, we will take her with us. Have a seat on the couch and I'll get the animals."

One of the police officers ushers the other officers outside before he sits on the edge of the coffee table, ready to ask questions and take notes. Mike comes out of the bedroom with Scooter under one arm and, to my surprise, Screamer under the other. I thought for sure the cat would hide from him. Mike passes her to me and I cuddle her to my chest as the officer and Mike exchange wary looks.

"Can you tell us what happened here tonight?" the officer asks.

I nod, hoping that I can, and then I swallow hard and proceed to tell them everything. At one point during my story, a female officer comes inside and whispers something in his ear. He makes a pained face, nods, and the woman goes back outside.

Once I'm done with the story, the officer takes all of my contact information and tells me, "We will place Mr. Allen under arrest after he's treated. The hospital personnel already know the situation and a guard will be stationed in his room until he's taken into custody, although I don't think he's going to be on the run anytime soon, judging by the wounds I saw. We will contact the sheriff's office in Charleston to let them know we have him. If his warrant is extraditable, they will come get him and he will face charges up there. Either way, we will keep you in the loop. Do you have any questions?"

"No."

"Okay, Ms. Allen, try to get some rest and we will be in touch."

I thank him and he steps away from us to make a phone call. Paxton came into the room during the discussion with the police officer and is standing off to the side with his arms crossed over his chest like he's guarding me.

"What about Carmen?" I ask quietly.

"I'll call and check on her and let you know," Mike says gently.

Screamer begins purring heavily, almost like she's trying to relax me, so I continue to hold her close and stroke her fur. About that time, Mike pulls his phone out of his pocket and answers it. I'm so lost in my head that I didn't even hear the buzzing in quiet mode.

"Wade," he says as he stands. "I'm going to take Scooter out. I'll be right back." He grabs the leash off the table and hooks it to his collar. Then they go out the front door and I turn back to the officer who is now off the phone and standing nearby.

"What now?" Now that everything is dying down and I've told them everything I know, I don't know what to do, or say, or what to expect. The best way to explain it is lost. I felt lost.

"Well, for now, you're safe. Billy-Jack Mullens was found dead in the woods. Your ex is in bad shape and under police supervision. You can rest easy tonight. As long as we have a way to contact you, you can go back to your life in Charleston, start a new one here, or move to Japan. That's your call. The point is, you shouldn't have any more issues."

"Thank you, officer."

He gives me a half smile like he's trying to be kind and leaves me with Screamer purring loudly.

# 15

# Stacey

Six weeks later...

The day after the showdown at Hudson's property I called my lawyer from Mike's house and he advised me to return to Charleston so I could secure everything in my name. Hudson apparently had some kind of trouble with that job he was on in Miami, which Mike didn't want to divulge at the time, and he wouldn't be home for another couple of days. I figured that was a sign from God that I should move on.

Although he warmed up to me in a real way at the end of my ordeal, I understand after all that he dealt with when it came to Carmen, he was in no hurry to get back into a relationship, especially one with a woman who had a ton of problems. I wrote him a letter to thank him and let him know why I left, and then I threw my stuff in my car and drove back.

Now I'm sitting in my car outside a group of townhomes on the Crystal River, waiting for Terri, the realtor, to show up. She's my friend's cousin who actually lives near Orlando, and she is doing me a favor by coming over here. A black Lexus SUV pulls up next to me and Terri steps out of the vehicle with a smile already on her face. Not the kind of smile that sleazy salesmen wear when they have dollar signs in their eyes, but the kind that's warm and honest. I breathe out a sigh of relief. It's amazing what a reassuring smile will do for me when my stomach is all knotted up with nerves.

Moving back here is what I wanted to do more than anything, but now that I'm here, I'm nervous. Hudson never called to check on me, or say he missed me, or even say '*screw you*.' It was radio silence from his end, so I'm sure he won't be happy to see me when he finally does. I'm not sure what I was expecting exactly, but complete silence was not it. We are both adults, though, and we can avoid each other to make it easier.

"Hi, I'm Terri," she offers as she reaches out to shake my hand.

"Stacey. Thanks for coming all this way."

"No problem, anything for Nicole. Let's take a look at this place."

We spend about 20 minutes going through the place with a fine-tooth comb and find minimal things to repair or change, and by the time we're done I'm ready to put in an offer. After my day spent on the water with Hudson, I've been obsessed with living on the water, and this little two-bedroom, two-bathroom condo is the perfect size for me. Now that I have access to the bank accounts again, I can afford it with no problem. I can already picture my time spent relaxing and reading on the screened-in back porch that overlooks a canal off the river.

Although the place is move-in ready, it will take two weeks for Compass Title to process the paperwork so I can close on the house. For now, I'm staying at the Plantation Inn and going in later this afternoon to meet with Mr. Clark to discuss working at the Lobster Lounge again.

———

AT 6:15 PM, I'm sitting in Mr. Clark's small office off of the kitchen, waiting for him to finish dealing with an unhappy customer. The walls are covered in yellow, aged signs with rolled-up corners for workers' compensation and minimum wage, which are stuck to the walls with various colored thumbtacks. His desk faces the wall and there are a few snapshots of his family thumbtacked to the board and one of him with his arm around Aerosmith lead singer, Steven Tyler, from his visit last year. The desk is cluttered in paperwork and discarded paperclips and I can't help but think about how disorganized all of this is. Mr. Clark returns and sits in the office chair, wiping his forehead with a handkerchief and settling his glasses back on his nose.

"Sorry about that, Stacey. Things have been a little crazy since you left. Doesn't seem to be a decent waitress who has applied. The current waitresses are all overworked and ready to string me up if I don't find them some help. I'm praying you came in to get your job back."

"Yes, actually I did. Now that I'm free and clear of my ex-husband, I can fill out all of the necessary paperwork and provide you with references and my résumé." I pass him the résumé and he takes it.

"You don't need to do all of that. I gave you a chance and you proved yourself without all of that. If you want the job, it's yours." He grows quiet for a minute as he studies the résumé.

"You have a college degree in finance?" he asks as he scratches his head a little.

"Yes, sir. I thought I told you that when I applied."

"You could have told me you were the queen of England and I wouldn't have cared at that point. You said you were in trouble and needed help and I was soft enough to give it a try. You know you could get a better job than here with a degree like that, right?"

"Yes, sir, I do. But I like it here. I love the town, the people, and I enjoyed this job."

I twiddle my thumbs a little, nervous that he'll tell me I'm overqualified now that he sees my work and education history. I always thought that was a stupid reason for not hiring someone.

"What if we discussed another option?"

"What kind of option?" I question, a little skeptical.

"What if you work part-time on the floor waitressing and part-time doing my accounting? I can't keep up with it." He gestures around the office at the mess and piles of papers. "That way, maybe I can actually take a vacation once in a while and eat dinner with my wife on occasion. Maybe even take my grandson fishing before he grows up, without worrying this place is going to fall apart."

"Wow. That's a lot to trust me with. Are you sure you don't want to think on that? I like waitressing here so that would be enough for me."

"Stacey, you have a college degree. Now use it. Otherwise, all that time and money was spent for nothing. I'll spend time training you two days a week to start and the other three you can waitress. If it turns out to be something you don't like or don't want to do, then you can waitress full-time, but I think you'll do fine and it'll help me so much."

"I'm flattered that you think enough of me to ask me this. Yes, I'd love to try this out. When can I start?"

"Tomorrow on the lunch shift would be good for waitressing. I'll have you a schedule for the rest of the week then. I think we can start training you on the books next Monday morning. How do you feel about that?"

"Perfect!" I jump to my feet, barely able to contain my excitement.

"Stacey, this is a small town, so I heard what went on out there that night. Are you doing okay?"

"I'm probably better than I've ever been. That night was

hard, one of the worst, but it ended a nightmare for me that had lasted several years."

"I'm not sure that big bodyguard of yours faired the same."

"Hudson?"

"Yeah, couldn't remember his name. I've seen him a few times since you left, and he was looking a little rough."

I'm not sure what to say to that. Mike told me the day I left that Carmen died, so I figured that might be what Mr. Clark is seeing in Hudson. I almost reached out to give him my condolences when I heard, but I figured if he wanted to talk to me, he would've called me. He never did, so today when I leave here, I'm going to get rid of this burner phone I've been carrying for the last eight months and get a smartphone again. There's no need to wait for something that isn't going to come.

## 16

## Hudson

Of course, as soon as I left Crystal River all hell broke loose. The whole reason I had Stacey at my place was to keep her out of harm's way, and instead it put her in the middle of Hell. Anything and everything that could have gone wrong did and I was four and a half hours away, guarding someone else's woman.

When Mike finally told me what happened, I lost my shit. It took me a few minutes to calm down to get the whole story. Thomas and I ran into complications during that job for Josiah Brown and were there longer than we expected. Mike didn't tell me everything that happened until I was finished with that job because he knew there was nothing I could do about it. Not to mention, he thought I'd have the chance to talk to Stacey when I came back, but he had no idea she was leaving town so soon.

Arriving back at my house, I found that she'd cleared all of her stuff out and left me a note. I always thought getting a Dear John letter from Carmen when she left the first time would have been so much better than not knowing anything, but after getting Stacey's letter, I have to disagree.

*Dear Hudson,*

*I can't thank you enough for providing me with a safe place to hide and people to look out for me. Because of you, Mike, and Paxton, I live to breathe another day. I wanted to wait around and thank you myself, but Mike said there were complications and you were delayed coming back. My lawyer advised me to go home and get everything straightened out, so that's what I'm doing. Thank you for everything. I owe you.*

*Sincerely,*

*Stacey*

I'M NOT sure what I was hoping for. Did I want to come home and live happily ever after with her in my shack in the woods? Did I even know her well enough for something like that to work? No, not after a week of time with her, most of which was spent in a difficult situation. It would have been a huge mistake, just like marrying Carmen so fast.

Complicating things further was Carmen's death. We don't have a county morgue here, so her remains had to be dealt with in a timely manner, and her mom was still sitting around the clock with her dad who was fighting for his life. To help Myrtle, I took care of everything and went to Alabama to help her through the funeral.

Summer, Mike's wife, called me every day that I was gone for the funeral, worried I might have a nervous breakdown, but in all honesty, I was a little relieved. It's probably wrong to feel that way, but Carmen wasn't living her life, in fact she was barely surviving it. She almost killed her father and she'd broken her mother's heart. There was no way she could stay clean, so we were all likely in for more of the same behavior had she lived. Now, I choose to believe she's found peace on the other side and I don't have to lose sleep worrying about what she's gotten herself into.

What I wasn't expecting in the middle of all of this was to be missing Stacey so much. Her smile, her wild hair, the attitude she would throw at me when she thought I was being an ass, the sweet soul she tried to keep hidden but that kept peeking out, and even that damn screaming cat. *Never thought I'd say I miss that cat, but I do.*

The good news for me is that I've gotten over other losses in my life and kept right on going. I'm hoping this won't be any different. If I can just figure out how to make that ache that Stacey left in my chest go away in the meantime, I will be doing great.

———

IT'S NOW BEEN two months since Stacey left, and Carmen died. Work has gotten busier, Thomas has started dating someone, and Summer is doing well, but on bed rest. Mike says she's super bored, which is making her cranky. Summer cranky? I find that hard to believe, but it must be true because he's taking her out to dinner and has asked me, Thomas, Simone, Shay and Paxton to go with them. I thought we'd go somewhere nice like Katch 22, but Mike says she's craving scallops from the Lobster Lounge. I've avoided the place since Stacey left, only going in there once or twice and only when Mike would make me go, so I'm not thrilled about it.

On my way to dinner, I stop by the Sodium Fishing Gear shop and see my friend Casey who owns the place. Of course, I pick up a new baseball cap with their logo on it and make plans to go fishing with him next week. Then I head to dinner with my friends.

Seven of us are seated at a table by the windows facing Kings Bay. Pink, orange and blue paint the sky in another one of Crystal River's beautiful sunsets. The menu is new and I'm going over my options when a familiar voice grabs my attention and my head snaps up.

"Hey, guys! How are y'all doing?" she asks everyone with a huge smile, avoiding eye contact with me.

*What is she doing here? I didn't know she came back to town. She mentioned several times she wanted to stay here once her troubles were all over, but I figured when she went back to South Carolina that was going to be the last I'd see of her.*

Everyone greets her and I sit dumbfounded with my heart practically pounding out of my chest. Stacey's hair is pulled up in a fluffy, curly ponytail and her skin is brown from time spent in the sun. She looks healthy and happy, even more beautiful than two months ago. Medium-sized silver hoop earrings dangle from her ears and a delicate silver necklace hangs around her neck. It must be my turn to order because suddenly everyone is quiet and staring at me.

"Um...could I get a Red Right Return on draft?" She nods but doesn't say anything further. Shay and Paxton are on the other side of me so once they give their order, she scurries off to the bar to put in our drink order.

"Did you guys know she was here?" I look to Mike and Summer who are seated directly across from me. They exchange a look and Summer speaks up. "Mike and I knew. We thought you'd be happy to see her. You've been sulky since she left. Did we misjudge the situation?"

I don't know the answer to the question. I want to be mad that they knew she was here and didn't tell me, but how can I be when she's actually here? She didn't look excited to see me, though, so I'm not sure how this will play out.

Unwilling to wait to find out, I scoot my chair back and stand, looking around the restaurant. I don't see her, so I stride to the bar. My heart is racing and my palms are itching. *When did I turn into an adolescent boy again?* Women haven't made me nervous in a very long time, but there was so much left unsaid between us when she took off. I never dreamed she would come back and now she's here in the same town, same building, at the same time as me.

"Is Stacey in the back?" I ask Nick, the crazy bartender.

"Are you Hudson?"

I nod.

He nods and says, "Yeah, she's in the back office."

I move through the kitchen to the little office I remember from my visit with Mr. Clark. This time there is no Mr. Clark, just Stacey standing with her back to the door. Her hands are over her eyes and she's alone and quiet.

"Stacey," I say quietly, hoping not to startle her.

She spins to face me, her eyes wide.

"Hudson."

"You're back?"

She nods slowly.

"For how long?" I take a step closer to her.

"Forever."

"Did you come back for me?" I take another step closer.

Her chin tilts up, a little defiant. "No, I came back for me."

"Did you even want to see me?"

"I don't know. Did you want to see *me*?"

"Yes," I answer, and I'm so close now I can feel her breath.

"You never called me," she says, and it's then that I can see the hurt in her eyes.

"I wasn't sure you wanted me to. You left town before I came back from Miami."

"I wanted you to."

Instead of saying something else, I close the distance between us and kiss her. She opens for me instantly and my tongue delves inside, slowly stroking hers as I wrap my arms around her and pull her close. We continue like that for what feels like only a second, but it must be a while because someone clears their throat behind me, breaking things up. Stacey tries to back out of my arms, but I continue to hold her tight against me.

"Stacey, you just got another table," Nick tells her on a chuckle.

"Okay, I'll be right out."

He laughs louder as he walks away.

"When can I see you?" I ask, not letting go until she tells me what I want to hear.

"I don't get off until after 10 tonight."

"Okay. I'll hang at the bar until your shift is over. Then you can come back to my place."

"I can't. I need to let my dog out."

"Dog?"

"Yeah, I bought a French bulldog puppy. How about if you come to my place?"

"No offense, but I'm not going to Crack Town. I'm done with that life."

"Don't be silly, I don't live over on Eighth Avenue anymore. I bought a condo on the river near Three Sisters Springs."

"Fine. I'll see you soon." I kiss her on the lips lightly and let her go. Then I make my way back through the kitchen to my table. There's no hiding the damn smile on my face and my friends, being the assholes they are, have no problem razzing me through the rest of dinner.

---

ONCE STACEY IS off of work, I follow her back to her place. A definite improvement from the shithole I first found her in. As soon as she opens the door, she's greeted by a small, high-energy set of ears moving at full speed toward her ankles. She bends down and scoops it up into her arms as she continues the rest of the way in.

"How's my sweet Nitro? How's my baby boy?" she coos to the tiny white dog.

"You named him Nitro?" She looks back at me over her shoulder like I'm nuts.

"Of course! Didn't you see how fast he is?" She cuddles him close for another minute before she asks me to grab his leash from the table. I grab it and turn just in time to catch sight of Screamer, her crazy cat, darting for the bedroom. *I guess it's going to take some time for her to get used to me again.*

Once Nitro has been out to do his business and we are stretched out on her couch, she reaches over and snatches the baseball cap off my head. "I see you got a new hat."

"How did you know?"

"You only wore two different hats when I was here before and both were SFG, which took me forever to figure out stood for Sodium Fishing Gear; neither of those looked like this."

"Casey got some new ones in stock and I was in the shop today, so I picked up a new one. I didn't realize you paid such close attention to me."

"You have no idea," she remarks on a sly smile.

Moving quicker than she expects, I twist around and pull her under me, and her legs automatically wrap around my waist. I stifle a groan and lean down to place a soft kiss on her forehead.

"What else did you notice?"

"That you have a small tan birthmark on your left butt cheek." She grins and it's cute.

"Oh really. What else?"

"That you only own Adidas shoes and athletic clothes. No Nike."

"And?"

"That you groan anytime I do this." She tilts her pelvis to press up against me harder, and I do in fact groan. *Shit, I didn't even realize that.*

"Want to know what I notice about you?"

"Yes." She smiles at me and I lean down to kiss her nose this time.

"I noticed that if you aren't out in public, you prefer to be barefooted and your toenails are always painted."

"This is true. What else?"

This time I kiss her chin and I can feel her shallow breaths warm against my face. She's so turned on right now she can't stand it.

"That you get turned on by just a little kiss. It doesn't even have to be a deep one. It can be any kiss," I pause and kiss the swell of her breast above the line of her tank top, "anywhere." This time I kiss her neck.

"I also noticed you love animals, probably more than people, and that your favorite author is likely Kaylee Ryan. You have several of her books and it looks like you've read them a hundred times each, judging by the wear and tear on them. And finally, I noticed that this spot, right here," I lean in to lick right behind her ear, "sends shivers through your body and tightens your nipples if I lick it just right."

"Hudson," her voice is breathy.

"Stacey."

"I've missed you," she confesses.

"Me too, babe." I lean in to kiss her right this time, showing her physically just how much I've missed her.

---

17

Stacey

---

It's been seven months since I came back to Crystal River and they have been the best of my life. It's Saturday afternoon and Hudson asked me to meet him at his place before we go to dinner for my birthday. We spend most of our time at my condo these days since he bought a boat, so I'm surprised by his request. It's winter here, which means that we get some cool weather. It's been unseasonably warm, so I'm in my shorts, a tank top and sneakers. I let myself inside with Nitro on the leash following close on my heels. On the table is a delicate white tulip in a vase tied with a pretty pink ribbon and the card in front of it that has my name written on it. I open it and read.

*Stacey,*
*Keep Nitro on the leash and walk down to the creek. I'll be waiting.*
*Hudson*

EXCITEMENT FILLS me and I set the card down and hurry out the door. No one has ever done anything like this for me. Don't get me wrong, in the beginning Lawson would buy me flowers, but he always just gave them to me with no creativity. Not only is Hudson being creative, it's obvious he's got something up his sleeve and the anticipation of what it could be is part of the excitement.

Nitro leads the way at the clipped pace of a puppy and we're down at the creek in record time. As soon as the clearing comes into view I'm dumbfounded. There are candles lit all over the place along the ground and sitting on the very low branches of the old oak trees that hang over the area. A pale blue blanket is spread out on the ground and a big brown picnic basket sits in the middle. Standing next to the blanket is Hudson in a pair of nice shorts, a polo shirt and sneakers. In his arms is a precious, dark gray French bulldog with bigger ears than even Nitro has and a big red bow around his neck. *What is going on?*

The closer we get, the more Nitro tugs and pulls on the leash. He can smell the other dog and he wants to meet it.

"Who do you have there?" My smile is uncontainable as I nod toward the adorable pooch in his arms.

"This is Remington. Happy birthday, babe." Hudson squats down and sets the puppy on the ground, now holding a leash I didn't notice before. The two pups sniff and circle each other until their leashes are all tangled up and we're struggling to straighten it all out.

"He's mine?"

"Yes, of course. A birthday present." Hudson's wearing his wide smile today. It's the same one that I now see all the time since I came back to town. He's clearly not the same man I met nearly eight months ago.

Once we have the puppies untangled and contained, each of us holding one of them, he tells me, "That's not exactly how

I wanted all of that to go, but I forgot to factor in puppy exuberance."

I move in close to kiss him hello and he captures my waist with one arm and lays a fantastic kiss on my lips. "I wanted to give you Remington and my heart at the same time."

I feel my whole face soften and my eyes well up with tears. "Your heart?"

"Yeah, my heart. I love you, Stacey, and I've wanted to tell you for a while, but I was always afraid of it being too soon."

"I love you too. I've known forever but didn't want to freak you out so I kept quiet."

He kisses me softly, with more feeling this time.

"Let's sit down and have dinner. I picked up sushi from World Fusion; I know it's your favorite. The boys can play while we eat."

"His name is Remington? Like the gun?"

"Yeah, I decided with ears like that he needed a masculine name and I wasn't sure what you'd come up with." He grins at me.

"Come here, Remmy," I coo as I pull him away from Nitro and snuggle him. Hudson digs the food out of the basket and I finally put Remmy back down again to play.

"This is the best birthday I've ever had," I blurt out, unable to contain my happiness.

"Although I'd love to be pleased that I'm giving you the best birthday you've ever had, I'm also a little pissed that no one before me has given you more."

"It's just perfect, that's all. What made you choose this spot?"

"I figured when I told you I love you, it should be in the spot where I first realized that I could love you. It's almost like the seed was planted here." He shrugs, seeming a little embarrassed by his reasoning.

"That makes it more special, thank you."

"I knew from the moment we got back together that I would be getting you another dog. You were deprived too long, and I know how much you love animals. I wanted to give him to you for Christmas but he was too little to leave his mom at that time, so I had to wait a couple more weeks. It just happened to work out perfectly."

"I love him and it seems Nitro does too." I glance over and the puppies are rolling around on the grass, chewing on each other and playing. "Screamer might not be quite so excited about it, but she'll get used to it."

"Hate to break it to you, babe, but that cat isn't excited about much."

We both laugh and go back to our lunch.

Within half an hour the food is cleared away and the puppies are finally passed out by our feet on the blanket. I'm curled into Hudson with my head on his chest and an arm thrown over his stomach. We're chatting about everything and nothing all at the same time when I decide to take advantage of the situation.

I slide up closer to his face. "What else do I get for my birthday?" I nip his chin and lay a chaste kiss on his lips. Then I slip my hand under his shirt and up his torso, tracing the ridges in his abs as I go. His eyelids grow hooded in an instant and his tongue snakes out to lick his lower lip. With a quick twist of his hips, he rolls me to my back and slides his big body between my thighs.

"What are you thinking?" He's grinning because he knows what I'm thinking and wants to hear me say it.

"I want a little outdoor lovin'. I've been thinking about it since that day back in the beginning when you brought me out here and almost jumped my bones."

"You have?"

"Duh!" I giggle and he closes the distance between us. Pressing his hips against me in the sweetest, most promising way, and I can tell he wants that too. The kissing begins slow and controlled and oh so sexy, but it doesn't take long to heat up. My moans seem to get swallowed up by the trees as he works his way down my neck to my breasts. His warm mouth surrounds my nipple, pulling gently, and I'm ready to get things moving so I tug at the waistband of his shorts, hoping to dislodge them from his hips. We got rid of condoms several months ago after I went on birth control and we both got tested. That night was probably the best sex of my life, but I love that now we don't have to pause when we're too frenzied to deal with that.

My eyes close as he switches breasts and I'm getting close just from his work at my chest, until he stops abruptly.

"Stace—" His voice is suddenly serious, and in that split second I worry I'll open my eyes to find the bear family watching us.

My eyes flash open but instead of bears I find puppies. Apparently, they don't sleep through moaning and begging.

"Damn," I mutter.

Hudson busts up laughing and I follow shortly after. We climb up and gather all of our stuff, spending the majority of the time blowing out and collecting the candles, and then we make our way back to Hudson's little house, where we spend the rest of the evening in bed, continuing the best birthday I've ever had.

Life is finally sweet for me and I thank God every day that Hudson saved me in more ways than one. I can't wait to see what the future holds for us.

## The End

Coming later this spring... Saving Simone. The story of Thomas Wade and Simone Sayer.

TO CONTACT TIFFANI LYNN, sign up for her newsletter or find more of her steamy reads visit Tiffanilynn.com

Made in the USA
Columbia, SC
25 February 2019